I used to Love Her

Aaron Bebo

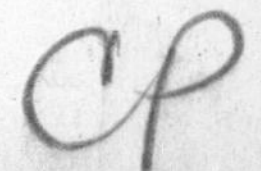

Published by:
G Street Chronicles
P.O. Box 1822
Jonesboro, GA 30237-1822

www.gstreetchronicles.com
fans@gstreetchronicles.com

Cover design: Dynasty's Cover Me Designs

Editor: Urban Editor

ISBN13: 978-1-9405749-7-4
ISBN10: 1940574978
LCCN: 2014935469

Join us on our social networks

Like us on Facebook: G Street Chronicles
Follow us on Twitter: @GStreetChronicl
Follow us on Instagram: gstreetchronicles

I used to Love Her

Acknowledgements

As always this book is dedicated to the unseen force that allows me to see and be a bit more creative in the world.

To my grandmother whom I still miss daily, I am still here proving them wrong. You keep watching over me.

To my mother, we're going away on a nice vacation somewhere this summer. So I can tell you how all this happened. As if you weren't there. Smiles.

To the wonderful Nene Capri Boss Lady INDEED!!!!!!!

To my entire G STREET FAMILY, Too many wonderful talents to name. I hope we all share the same intent.

To all my long time supporters and new supporters, please continue this journey with me as I walk from one door to the next. I thank you all for your support.

To the Boss Man himself Big George Sherman and the First Lady Shawna, I thank you for offering me this wonderful opportunity. I am definitely ready to pick up my shoes. LET'S DO THINGS MAJOR!!!!! Thank you again.

Finally to my Spoiled Apple that never goes bad Kenisha Parker & The Bad Apple Cru…

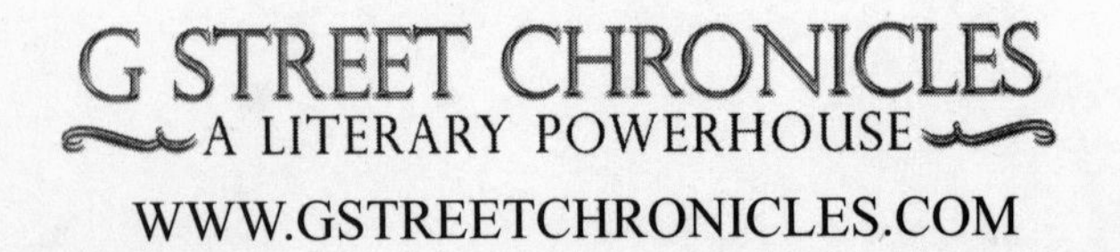
G STREET CHRONICLES
A LITERARY POWERHOUSE
WWW.GSTREETCHRONICLES.COM

PROLOGUE

"You want to end shit? 'Cause I'm good with that!"

"Good. I wouldn't want this coming to an end to interfere with our real business."

"Okay, cool. I'll be on the first flight out tomorrow."

He drained his cup, set it on the nightstand, and turned over to go to sleep.

"There is one other thing."

"What?" he asked not bothering to turn around.

She picked up an envelope from the nightstand on her side of the bed.

"I think you should read this."

He rolled over, snatched the envelope from her hand, and tore it open. He pulled the papers from the envelope and started reading. As he did, Dana got out of the bed and headed toward the bathroom.

She paused and said over her shoulder, "Kiss the wifey for me when you get back home."

He couldn't believe what he was reading. He jumped up from the bed.

"What the fuck is this?"

He heard the shower water running, but got no response. He knew she had heard him. He barged into the bathroom, opened the shower door, and pushed the papers toward her.

"What the fuck is this?" he demanded.

She looked at him and frowned.

"What does it look like? I'm pregnant."

Trey felt his temperature rising.

"Well, whose is it because we ain't been fuckin' like that."

"Haven't we?"

She turned off the water and stepped around him as she got out. She grabbed a towel and dabbed at her body as she walked back into the bedroom. Trey was right on her heels waving the wet paperwork.

"I ain't goin' out like that."

He tossed the papers onto the floor, stormed over to the bed, and lay on his back staring at the ceiling.

"I know, right. You went all in. Got that juice on you and tried to merc sumthin'. You the one who stopped putting baggies on. I am carrying your child."

"C'mon, ma. You know better than that shit you talkin'. I ain't even on it like dat. You know I already got my wifey. We can't have none of dat whut you talkin'."

She walked over to the bed and gently traced a finger along his hair line with a manicured nail tip.

"Talkin'. We both exchanged some words, nigga. You knew the dos and don'ts and so did I. You broke a promise to yourself. You said you would never get caught up on this thing of ours. I gave you what you wanted. I'm what I told you I was always, a tiger, Panthera tigris. You had your chance to back out. You didn't."

She looked at the TV screen and said, "Oh, look, my favorite part."

Sharon Stone stood in a huge walk-in closet surrounded

by designer names and Robert De Niro presented her with an assortment of jewels.

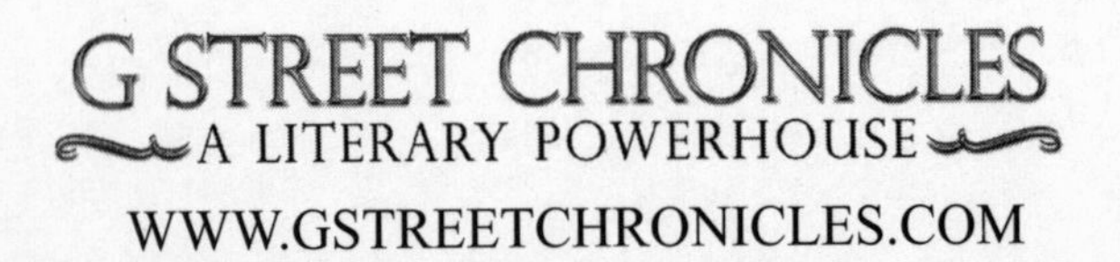
G STREET CHRONICLES
A LITERARY POWERHOUSE
WWW.GSTREETCHRONICLES.COM

CHAPTER 1

A Teenage Love

Tina rolled out of bed when she heard her grandmother moving around the house. As she rose, she looked at the clock on the night stand and then at the shape beneath her comforter. Tina stepped out her room into the hallway just as her grandmother was coming out of her bedroom.

"Hey, Grandma."

Mrs. Daniels cut her eyes at Tina and grunted before taking the few short steps into the kitchen. Her grandmother knew she had been sneaking Trey into the house at night. Tina stepped quickly behind her.

"I think Mrs. Jackie upstairs hit that number she been telling you to play, that four zero five."

Mrs. Daniels turned the water on in the sink and rinsed out her coffee cup. The kitchen was a tight fit. All she had to do was turn and she could reach out to turn the flame on under the kettle. She put the cup in the middle of the cooker, reached up to the cabinet above the stove, and pulled down the Folgers. That was the only brand of coffee she would drink.

Mrs. Daniels had been sipping on the two seeded fruit since the age of five. Her own grandmother would share cups of the steamy liquid with her like treats when she was a young girl. Mrs. Daniels drank a minimum of four cups a day.

"Four zero five. I knew I should've put five dollars on it 'stead of three." Mrs. Daniels said as spooned the instant crystals into her cup.

"You hit the number, Grandma. How much do three dollars pay?"

Tina was relieved her grandmother had hit the number. Her grandmother might have said something to her about Trey being in the house. Tina had snuck him in well past the visiting curfew her grandmother had set. She was more than sure her grandmother had heard Trey and her in the wee hours of the morning. Tina had seen the kitchen light come on just as Trey had pushed deep causing her to whimper and the headboard to knock against the door, the same door that would have opened to the kitchen had her bed not been positioned the way it was.

Tina had dug her nails into his arms and whispered, "My grandmother's in the kitchen."

Trey had looked up at the light creeping through the crack at the top of the door and continued to grind inside her slowly.

"Mmm...."

Tina couldn't wait to get back into bed with her baby.

"If it came straight that should be thirty two hundred. I sure hope that young boy got that kinda money."

"Grandma, he gonna have the money. He be writing for Mr. Jesse, Keisha's granddaddy. You know Mr. Jesse," Tina said.

Tina's grandmother always tried to pretend like she

was naïve to anything outside of her favorite shows, Falcon Crest and Dynasty, and whatever was happening at her job at the hospital.

"Oh… so you know that boy?"

The boy to whom Mrs. Daniels was referring to was a neighborhood kid named Dennis. He lived in the same apartment complex they did, 840 Grand Concourse. Dennis had even been to their apartment a few times. He'd come to drink bottles of E & J brandy with Tina and her sister, Michell. Dennis often ran to the grocery store behind the apartment building for Mrs. Daniels. Tina was sure her grandmother knew exactly who Dennis was because she wouldn't pull out a nickel in front of a stranger. Mrs. Daniels had given him money to play the street number on several occasions.

Like most old folks who played the numbers in the neighborhood, she had hopes of getting an extra buck or two without seriously breaking the law. Although the street numbers were illegal, it was a tradition in the neighborhood. The numbers were not frowned on by most of the elders in the community that indulged in the poor man's hustle. Hitting for the thirty-two hundred had been a blessing for her grandma.

Mr. Jesse always paid out. Tina knew that. So did her grandmother. Mrs. Daniels was implying something else.

"You want me to get the money from Dennis for you, Grandma?" Tina asked.

Mrs. Daniels lifted the kettle from the fire just as it was about to scream and poured the hot water in her coffee cup.

"You think you goin' see him today?" Mrs. Daniels asked.

Tina was feeling braver than she had when she first

came into the kitchen and her nerves began to calm since she knew that her grandmother wasn't going to go crazy about Trey being in her bed. She was pretty sure that her grandmother knew he was there, but Mrs. Daniels didn't seem inclined to cause a ruckus about it today.

Even though Mrs. Daniels didn't care for Trey, she did allow him to visit Tina in the house, in her room, as long as it was a decent hour. It was Tina who had come up with the idea of pretending to walk him to the door farewell while he waited in her room.

Mrs. Daniels' always closed her room door by 9 O'clock which was perfect for Tina's scheme. Tina would never have been able to pull this off had her grandfather still been alive. Hell, Trey probably wouldn't have been allowed into the house after 9 o'clock at night.

"Grandma, give me the ticket and I'll have the money for you by the time you get home from work."

Mrs. Daniels dipped her left hand into the pocket of the burgundy robe Tina had given her for Christmas and pulled out a small, yellow slip. It was the type of memo paper used in offices. She handed the slip to Tina.

Tina looked at the slip. The number *405* was scribbled on it and the letters *DEN* appeared beneath the number.

"If you get the money, I need you to take six fifty to the rent office. If that boy come over here today, see if he'll run to the grocery store. I got the taste for some cabbage this weekend. And, grab a few other things."

A few other things! That was a joke! Tina cooked most of the meals anyway. She always did the shopping. The mention of 'that boy' reminded her that Trey was only a few yards away curled up under her blanket like a baby.

Tina was used to her grandmother referring to anyone younger than herself as 'boy' or 'girl'. It was the way she said it when she referred to Trey that set her teeth on edge. Her grandmother couldn't stand him and the tone of her voice when she referred to Trey let Tina know it.

Trey, the love of Tina's life, was tall '6 1" with light-brown skin. He had a gorgeous smile, but Tina loved him for his mind. Trey was smart – really smart – and creative. His gift was the written word. Trey wanted to be a songwriter and a rapper. She understood his dream; and recognized his ambition. Other people didn't understand but Tina did. Trey was going to be the best rapper alive.

*****

Trey stirred in the queen sized bed before his eyes popped open to the darkness of the room. He blinked a few times before the sliver of light from the kitchen allowed him to make out the familiar shadows in the bedroom.

He heard the muffled voices in the kitchen and realized that Mrs. Daniels was awake. It had to be at least 6:30 a.m. on Tuesday morning. He had to meet Boogs around four o'clock to go to a meeting with Fogg, their producer.

One of the A&R's at the Global Entertainment Group who was handling the Annie Oakley project had heard their demo and wanted to meet them. He had chosen one of Fogg's beats to be on Annie's follow up. They were set to meet her for a studio session later that evening.

Trey reached toward the nightstand on the left side of the bed. He felt the pack of Newport's just as the bed creaked from his movements. He pulled his fingers back quickly thinking again about his early morning craving for nicotine. That would have to wait, at least until after Mrs. Daniels left for work. Tina wanted him to quit smoking anyway. *Maybe I should quit,* he thought and then stretched his hand out to pick up his Styrofoam cup from the nightstand. Trey leaned up on one arm and tilted the cup to his lips draining it of its syrupy contents. Then, he lay still trying to hear the conversation going on in the next room. The lights on the stereo across the room started to blur before his eyes and the barely audible sound from the speakers began to echo in his ears. Trey drifted away in a Promethazine with codeine haze.

*****

"Did you ever get those boots you were telling me about?" Mrs. Daniels asked stirring her coffee.

She was referring to the riding boots Tina had been talking about for the last week. She had first seen the boots in a small shoe shop on Chambers street. Tina was on her way home from school, the Borough of Manhattan Community *College when* she saw the boots in the shop window. She couldn't resist walking into the small shop where she was greeted by the smell of leather and an older white man with snow white hair. The man peered over top of the wire-rimmed glasses with thick lenses that obscured his pupils. The man approached Tina with a bright smile and extended his right hand which was shaking.

"How are you young lady? What can I help you with today?"

"Hey, I was interested in the boots right there."

Tina pointed to the riding boots in the window with her left hand and took the frail hand the old man was offering with her right.

The old man seemed to stumble forward a few feet gracefully to look at the boots she had pointed out. He looked back over his left shoulder at her and glanced at the white Reebok Classics on her feet.

"What are you? About a seven in little boys?" the old man said as he stepped back and curled his index *finger* over his shoulder.

"Come. I'll get the boots for you so you can try them on."

She followed the old man protesting weakly, "No, I don't want to buy them now. I was just wondering if my size was available. I really like them but I can't afford them today."

The clumsily arranged displays mad it hard for her to maneuver around the shop. She spotted a cute pair of red pair of pumps as she finally stepped into an open aisle. The old man had stopped in the aisle as well.

"Have a seat, young lady. How can you know if your size is available if you don't try on the boot?"

He directed Tina to a short stool about three feet wide with a black cushion on top.

"Take off your shoes. I will bring back an eight. You see, these boots have a funny arch, ahh, never mind," the old man continued pushing his palms out in front of him at the air, "I'll bring the right boot for you. Just have a seat."

Tina watched him walk away. She set her Jan Sport next to the stool and sat down. She unlaced her tennis shoes and slid her feet out of the comfortable leather of the Classic. She looked down at her feet and wiggled her toes in the fabric of her yellow socks. Tina thought about the day she and Jarod had gone out to Coney Island. They had walked through the sand sharing their thoughts.

The old man seemed to appear out of nowhere holding a large box with the top open. He offered her the box with a smile and a nod. Tina took the box, removed one of the boots, and set the box next to her book bag. She examined the boot. She had not noticed that on the display.

"There's no zipper?" She said.

"This boot is fixed with an elastic sheet stitched on the inside of the leather around the mid calve area. So you only need to worry if your foot is comfortable."

The leather felt good in her hands. It was definitely of high quality, not the cheap, low-grade stuff used for knock off purses and other accessories. Tina slipped her foot into the boot and slid it over her calf easily. She stood up and took a few steps. It was the most comfortable boot she had worn in her life.

"It feels great. These are an eight?" Tina asked taking a few more steps before returning to the stool.

The old man smiled and said, "Yes, it is an eight. It fits good, no?"

"Yes, it fits very well. I didn't even know I wore an eight."

"You don't wear an eight. You wear seven," the old man said pointing at the Reeboks, "but, in this boot, you wear an eight."

"How did you know I wear a seven?"

"If a man knows your shoe size at a glance, he can make you Cinderella," the old man said with a smile.

She didn't understand his answer. She returned his smile.

Tina wiggled her toes as she opened the refrigerator and passed Mrs. Daniels the can of Carnation milk.

"No, Grandma, I didn't get the boots. They are so nice. You gotta see them. I gotta have 'em by the time me and Chell go to the winter resort up in Lake Georgia."

"Chile, you probably wear them boots once or twice and they will get lost in that room somewhere. What happened to the hat, coat, and gloves set I bought you that time? I don't even see that no more, all that money I spent on them coats for you girls."

Tina laughed.

"Grandma, those were sheepskin coats. They only came back in style for a minute. That was two years ago."

"Since when a coat come with an expiration date? You chillen kill me, act like money grow on trees," Mrs. Daniels said stirring the milk in her coffee.

She lifted her cup to her lips and took a sip. The steam rose from the cup causing her to squint her eyes.

"Umm. Well, you go head and get them boots for your trip. If I don't get 'em, I know that boy ain't going give you no four hundred dollars."

"Grandma, Trey spends money on me. What about the trip to Nassau?"

"You mean the one where I had to wire you six hundred dollars for a plane ticket back after y'all got to fighting and he kicked you out the hotel? Chile, you better wake up. This is New York, the city of dreams. That boy just another young, black boy without a pillow."

Mrs. Daniels shook her head as she walked past her granddaughter. Tina waited until her grandmother went back into her room and closed the door before she opened the refrigerator and pulled out a carton of eggs and a package of sliced American cheese. She placed the eggs and cheese on top of the metal table that set against the door that would have lead into her room.

She peeped up at the crack at the top of the door and smiled before turning back to the icebox and removing a package of Hillshire Farm Polish Kielbasa, a red onion, and a green pepper. She placed them on the table with the eggs and cheese and walked back to her room.

Tina stepped into the room and heard the voice of

'The Geek,' former rapper turned radio personality, and the slick jingle for FLY 97's morning show. The sun had started to pierce through her window curtain. She could see Trey's tight, fit six-pack as he lay there on the bed on his back with a Newport tucked between his lips and his right hand stuffed in his boxer shorts.

The sun also made visible the scar that ran along his left cheek, the result of a brawl at a show he did at The Empowers' Castle. That was same night Tina had met him.

Trey was in the E.R. at St. Luke's and Tina was passing through back when Mrs. Daniels was working nights.

Trey was pressing a ball *of* cotton to his cheek when he reached out and pinched the hem of her tennis skirt attempting to get her attention. At once, Tina noticed the bloody fingerprint he left.

"What are you doing?" she said sharply.

"I was trying to see what type material a Goddess wears."

Trey's long eyelashes eclipsed his dark pupils. His eyes seemed hard and cold. They held a hint of compassion, but no trace of an apology.

Tina noticed the blood running down from beneath the wad of cotton. Blood ran along the fingers of his left hand down his palm and wrist, around to the back of his hand.

"What happened to you?" she asked him and immediately wondered to herself, Why do I care?

"A brawl at the Castle tonight. Some dude cut me, for initiation into some gang probably, but I wasn't leaving there until that promoter up the bread for our performance."

He stuffed his right hand in his pocket and pulled out a decent size poke.

"Sev fifty. My boys disappeared on me, but I took one

for the team," he said as he pushed the bills back into his pocket.

"You were performing there tonight? That's crazy. Me and my girl were supposed to go to the Castle tonight but her ride fell through. She's real cool with Scheme."

"Scheme, oh, word?"

Tina sat in the vacant seat next to him. She wasn't a bit surprised at his reaction to her mention of Scheme. He was the biggest thing in hip-hop right now.

"So, what's your name?" Tina pulled a package of Kleenex from her Coach bag and continued, "Here let me see that."

Tina pulled his hand away from his face. The minute she did she wished she hadn't. The gash was deep. She could see the inside of his mouth. Blood was pouring out of the gaping hole. She pressed a wad of Kleenex against his cheek and winced.

"It's that bad?"

She nodded.

"So, what's your name?"

"Jarod."

"Jarod! I thought you said you were performing at the Castle tonight?"

"I did."

He reached up to press his fingers against the Kleenex between hers.

"I got it."

"So, who are you? Mic Jarod a mo'?" she said laughing.

She removed her fingers from the Kleenex and nudged her shoulder against his playfully. She was close. He could smell cinnamon on her breath and citrus in her hair.

"Oh, you got jokes. Naw, my stage name is Trey Eight."

Tina stayed in the E.R. with him until he was stitched

up at 5:30 in the morning. They left St. Luke's and went to an all-night frank and papaya joint on Broadway.

They talked all night. Trey shared his aspirations to be a rapper. He was determined to get as far away as he could from the apartment he shared with his grandfather in Harlem. Tina confessed her interest in the business side of the music industry. She wanted to manage talent and handle contracts.

Trey was part of the Hustle Kingz which was made up of himself, his partner, Boogs, and their producer, Fogg. They were currently seeking management.

"We 'bout to blow. I wish you woulda been there last night so you could've seen how crazy muthafucka muthafuckas went when I did my verse to Fly by Night. That nigga, Scheme, ain't even get to perform. I shut dat shit down!" he said before taking a big bite out of a chili dog with the works.

Tina wondered how he was able to chew. They had just put two hundred and twenty stitches in his left cheek stitching from the inside out.

She had heard *Fly by Night*. It had been on the Midtown Show Down segment of the afternoon show on FLY 97. It had won eleven weeks straight, if she wasn't mistaken. Tina liked the song.

"Which one are you?"

"What?"

"On the song. Which part is yours?"

"You heard the joint?"

Dimples formed in her caramel cheeks when she smiled.

"Several times."

"I love ya smile."

"It's already engaged to my lips," she said widening

her grin.

"What's that?"

She pointed at the screen behind the counter. Jenny Choi from Channel 4 News was reporting live from a Trenton, New Jersey neighborhood.

"Police have finally confirmed the Bentley you see behind me…"

The camera angle changed to show a pearl-white Bentley sitting awkwardly on the sidewalk in front of some apartments.

"…was carrying platinum rap artist Scheme, whose real name is Jesse Caldwell, and a female companion, Crystal Curry. The rapper was gunned down with his female passenger and chauffer while his Bentley idled near the curb. It is unclear why the rapper was in this area when he owns a home in Wayside, New Jersey. The rapper was scheduled to perform at The Emperor's Castle, a Mid-Town night club in New York City last night, but a brawl that preceded his performance caused the rapper to cancel the show…"

"Oh, my God," Tina said as she brought her left hand up to her mouth.

"What? I mean that's fucked up. Dude was nice and all but, hey, shit happens. I'm 'bout to fill his spot. , you can be my fan," he said with a smile.

Trey studied her face. Her eyes were filled with tears and her bottom lip quivered.

"What's wrong, shortie? Was you really that big of a fan?"

"That was my friend. The girl that was with him, Crystal. She went to the show...," her voice trailed off.

Trey reached across the table and took her hand.

"Damn, shortie. I'm sorry to hear that, really. It might

be a good thing you didn't go to the show. They might have been mentioning you like ya girl on some groupie shit."

She pulled her hand away from his. She was furious at him for his last comment about groupie shit. Crystal was her friend.

Crystal had been her homie since middle school. Crystal was the girl she had forgiven for stealing her two hundred dollars she was supposed to use to go on their senior trip, the bestie who had slept with, and gotten pregnant by, her sister's boyfriend. Tina had even convinced Michell to forgive her.

Now, she had gone and gotten herself killed. That must have been right after Crystal had called and told her something had happened to Scheme's Bentley and he couldn't pick them up. Crystal was supposed to be at home having a threesome with a spoon and a pint of Ben & Jerry's but she was dead. Tina reached up and touched the stitching on Trey's cheek.

"I don't want to be your groupie. I want to be your manager."

That was eighteen months ago. Trey and Tina could be found together every day after that. She met his friends and partners in rhyme, Boogs and Fogg. Fogg didn't really rap. He was the producer. Tina loved their music. Fogg played his own notes while everyone else was mostly using samples. Boogs was the funny one of the crew and a good rapper, too. Trey was, by far, the better rapper out of the two. They had created a small buzz around the city and a few places around the Tri-State area. When Tina started managing them, she got them signed to a single deal for a song titled, Pose for the Picture but the label folded three months after the single's release.

Trey was amazing. His concepts and delivery of song were so profound. She didn't like the fact that he smoked cigarettes but she hated the fact that he sipped syrup.

Tina noticed the smile pasted on Trey's lips as he lay in bed fondling himself. She saw the Styrofoam cup turned over on the nightstand as she stepped in the room and closed the door behind her. Tina crawled onto the bed like a cat stalking its prey, moving on her palms and knees until she hovered over Jarod.

She placed a kiss on his lips And said, "You ready for today? I think this is it."

"I'm always ready. I just hope this dude ain't no snobby office type tryin' to front like he know what hip-hop is."

"Naw, baby. I think this is going to be different. Global's hurting since Scheme got murdered. They got Annie Oakley but I know for a fact Scheme wrote most of her shit. Y'all can go over there and kill 'em!"

"We'll see," he said pulling the cigarette from his lips.

"You got this."

Tina heard the double bolt on the front door. Her grandmother was off to work. She started in on Trey right away. She freed him from his boxers and stroked his manhood. He swelled from her touch as blood filled his organ. The syrup had him in a dreamland and her touch only intensified his high.

Tina looked at him with a seductive look as her tongue teased the head of his cock. She jerked the skin near the head of his dick squeezing just a little before she took him into her mouth. Her mouth watered as her lips and tongue went to work on the head of his dick. His knees knocked as his legs locked together stiffly.

Tina spread his legs and ran her nails along his inner thigh. She tickled his sac with her fingertips while her other hand stroked his rising jones. She got on her knees and positioned herself between his legs so she could watch him. Her spit ran down his shaft making it shine like a trophy.

Trey could barely keep eye contact. He would look at her and then shove his head back against the pillow squeezing his eyes shut. Trey saw visions of purple flowers dancing in front of his eyes at those moments. Tina always won the stare downs when they were in this position.

Trey groaned as her nails softly raked his sac and the head of his dick scratched her throat. He balled his fist and beat them onto the mattress. He couldn't take anymore of her oral assault.

Trey lifted Tina up to free himself from her burning hot tongue. She sucked hard holding on like a bull terrier until he was able to wiggle free. Tina wiped her mouth and smiled.

"I always get the standing ovation. I'm nice on the mic," she said laughing.

His member was standing at full attention weaving back and forth like a cobra preparing to strike. He caught his breath before he got up and pushed her down to the mattress. He stroked his eager cock as he lifted her left leg and eased himself between her thighs.

He held her leg in the crook of his right arm and guided himself with his left until he felt his head enter her hot juices. He saw the lines in her forehead form as he began to drive his stiff log inside her. He pressed his left palm to the mattress and started to give her a serious pounding.

Tina felt him moving deep in her spreading her wide. She bit down on her lip and moaned his name loudly as he touched her stomach. Her body was on fire. Tina reached out and gripped the sheets as he pounded into her. Sweat dripped from her lids mixing with the tears of joy in her eyes. A bolt of fire shot up her spine before her entire body released and she screamed.

"Treyyyy! Oh, my gawd, I love you."

Trey released her leg and rolled her onto her stomach. He pushed her legs apart with his knees and grabbed a fist full of her hair, snapping her neck back as he pushed deep inside her.

"This my pussy?"

"Yes."

"I can't hear you. Who pussy is this?"

"It's yours. You know it's yours."

"You sure?"

"Yesss…"

She had released again. She shook with violent pleasure as her moisture formed like thick foam at the end of a wave. She could hear her wetness every time he crashed into her fiery abyss. It wasn't long before he too was overcome by pleasure and erupted like a volcano. They lay glued together in their sweat loving the moment.

Chapter 2

Stay Dat Bitch!

Dana stepped out of the black Rolls and onto the curb. Her personal body guard, Skarz, blocked the sun's light as he came to stand at her right side. A huge metal globe surrounded by sprinklers shooting water twenty feet into the air sat in front of the sixty-eight story building that housed the offices of G.E.G. the largest music distributor and record label in the United States. Dana and Skarz started up the marble steps and a fine mist touched Dana's face. .

Dana was the senior A&R and marketing advisor for the Urban Music Division. Her brown Joan and David Evensen Oxford heels beat at the polished granite floor as she entered the building and headed for the elevators. She gave curt nods to everyone that spoke to her.

When Dana first entered this building five years ago, she was a nervous wreck. She had made a name for herself as Dana Delight at FLY 97 radio. She had hosted the 'Traffic Jam' segment of the show that ran from 3P.M. to 7 P.M. She had a great time working at the radio station. It had given her the chance to get up close and personal with music stars and some great industry people. Dana used those connections to get closer to the offices with the million dollar budgets.

She attended every major industry event. It was radio that had allowed her to meet and start managing Scheme. She promoted the feisty Brooklyn Emcee every chance she got on the radio after their first chance encounter. Soon she met Darell Price at an after party for an R&B singer. He invited her to lunch the next week and offered her a position at G.E.G. It took her a few years to get herself established at the label. As soon as she did, she brought Scheme over and he gave her that final spark she needed.

Dana checked her appearance in the reflection of the marble walls near the elevators while she waited. The brown cashmere skirt and blazer she chose was cute but she was hoping the silk rust colored blouse with the plunging neckline would do all it was designed to do.

She was having a meeting with the vice president and president of the label. She was trying to convince them to give her a budget and allow her to launch a separate subsidiary division for hip- hop at the label. At present, all hip hop was distributed through the Urban Music Division.

She stepped off the elevator on the 50th floor and walked down the corridor to the conference room on the right. She reached out with her right hand for the medium sized chestnut leather saddleback leather satchel Skarz was carrying.

"Wait here," Dana said as she took the satchel and twisted the door knob.

Everyone looked up from the large conference table when Dana entered the conference room. Paul Lanno, the chairman of the label, was sitting at the head of the conference table wearing a well-tailored, black silk suit and the huge gold ring he always wore on his right ring finger. An article in GQ about the mogul had mentioned that he never went anywhere without the ring which was worth an estimated 2.7 million dollars.

The black diamond in the ring's face was almost five karats. Dana felt a warm chill as his eyes roamed her chest. She smiled and stepped further into the room. Darell Price clapped his hands together and walked toward her wearing a big smile.

"Dana, how you doing? Mr. Lanno, this is the star I was telling you about. She turned our Urban Department around in six months. Dana, meet your boss and mines, Mr. Lanno."

"How are you, sir?'

Dana moved toward the vacant seat next to Mr. Lanno. She set her satchel on the table and opened it to remove several folders. After she had arranged the paperwork on the table, she locked eyes with Mr. Lanno and offered her hand which he accepted with a sure smile.

"What I have here are the reports from last quarter sales and earnings. Rock, Heavy Metal, Urban Contemporary, R&B, and Rap. Judging from these numbers, I feel that we may need to concentrate more of our energies on marketing geared toward the hip-hop genre of music."

Dana began passing out the folders of paperwork. Of the nine people in the room, she and Darell were the only black faces. She hadn't even acknowledged Huey Lincoln, the vice president, or Roy Stevens, the label's president. There was no need to pitch to them now.

The white faces studied the paperwork before them, all except Mr. Lanno. He was checking Dana out. She watched him in her periphery while she explained the figures in the reports and pitched. The figures Dana presented supported her argument that it would be in their best interest to let her head up a new department directed toward marketing and promoting hip-hop. The biggest part of her pitch was the sixty four million dollar budget she wanted to start the division.

The best assets in her pitch was Annie Oakley, a fairly new artist signed to the label who had sold four million records in five months and had just wrapped up a European tour. Dana had brought Annie to the label and had personally handled the direction of her project. She was also Annie's legal guardian. The kicker was that Dana owned the publishing rights to the album Scheme had turned in before his death and the label needed that album.

Paul leaned forward and placed his hands on top of the table at her mention of the budget number. She noticed his index finger shoot up toward the ceiling.

"You have a question, Mr. Lanno?" Dana asked turning to look at him directly.

Lanno looked like he was in his mid-forties. His salon haircut was precise and clearly done by practiced hands. His face was shaven close enough to form a light shadow on his cheeks, so light that it didn't disturb the sun's kiss on his skin. His grey eyes were piercing and seemed to be undressing her as he gazed at her.

"Mr. Lanno?" Dana repeated.

She could see out of the corner of her eye Darell and a few of the other executives shifting in their seats.

This perverted playboy with the big wallet had all these people scared to address him, like he was some God; but, she knew the truth. This bastard probably listened to alternative music, if any at all. He was too busy traveling the world and screwing models on Lear jets. He didn't have a clue as what went into marketing music. He had inherited this company three years ago after his father died while on a mountain climbing expedition in the Canadian Alps over Lake Louise. When Dana first came to work for the company, Paul wasn't even an employee.

"I'm sure your dissertation is going to be flawless. Just get to the main point as to why I should give you sixty-four million dollars of my money?" Paul Lanno said flashing a charming smile.

"Let's look at our biggest competitor in the states, A.B.J. records."

Dana reached into her satchel and removed more papers. Dana pointed a manicured nail at the chart on the first page and turned the paper so that only Mr. Lanno had a clear view.

"We were in a bidding war with A.B.J. for a hip-hop based group, Land Pirates. We lost the war."

Dana shot a look at Darell before returning her gaze back to the sheet she held.

"Anyway, around the same time A.B.J. signed Land Pirates and their main act over there, Slither, a metal band two time Grammy winners. Well, lead singer Calvin Scarsfield decides he wants to eat his pistol. The label president gets a list of the roster on the label which was primarily metal and alternative rock. Looks over the list and selects the name Land Pirates thinking it was another metal band and put Slither's budget behind them."

She paused.

"They made the label three hundred million by the end of the closing quarter. Their album was released in the beginning of the third when label chairman, Kurt Strauss, was interviewed for TIME magazine earlier this year."

She removed a copy of the magazine with the Strauss on the cover and flipped through the pages.

"Here's what Kurt had to say concerning hip-hop and its' selling power, 'The saving face of our label after the loss of Calvin Scarsfield was a rap group the label had just acquired named Land Pirates.' He went on to say, 'Had this group been given a traditional budget for rap groups, the label may have just recouped what we put into the project.'"

She looked up from the article at the faces around the table. Her eyes came to rest on Mr. Lanno; before turning her attention back to the article.

"'I fucking love hip-hop!' I quote him. This is printed in TIME magazine excluding the expletive of course. If a seventy year old Caucasian man can see the effects this music can have on business when given the proper attention, I say we get on board or go from being the music industry leaders to following in the footsteps left by our competitors."

Paul nodded and said, "One more thing. What can you tell me about the status on Scheme's publishing? Are there going to be any delays with the album? We need to get that out there to the people ASAP, before the next big star appears"

Dana smiled.

"No worries there. I'm going to bring you the next big star. But I don't think anything should hinder the project at all. Hopefully, when we drop the album the press will bring up the murder investigation and let people know the new album is out."

"I like the way you think. My money might just be secure in your hands."

"Safer than Bank of America. I took up the position I did with Scheme because I knew him personally and I knew with my direction on the project it would push it toward the proper marketing avenues to make the label money."

Mr. Lanno smiled. He picked up the folder Dana had placed in front of him and tossed it into the middle of the long conference table causing the papers to spread across the table.

"And, it did. You did. Give her what she wants. Arrange a party announcing it. Invite the city. You," Paul said pointing his finger at Darell.

He continued speaking to Dana, "I want a thirty percent profit margin in the next quarter. Let's do lunch next week. Have Darell contact me at your convenience. I need at least twenty four hours to make reservations."

Mr. Lanno stood signaling the meeting was adjourned.

He headed out the conference room with everyone else on his heels leaving Dana and Darell alone.

"So, Darell, did you ever get that gardener?"

Dana had a very short affair with Darell when she first came to the label. He had invited her to the home in the Hamptons, the home he shared with his wife during the summer months.

Dana had found out he was married months after her visit, but three minutes of their attempt at intercourse she learned that Darell couldn't stand up to what she was offering. He had messed himself on her leg while trying to find her entrance. It was a shame, too. It looked like he might have a good piece of equipment. Dana's quip about the gardener came from the fact that she had caught his neighbor peeping through the window at her while she straddled him on his wife's Italian leather sofa, the one he and his wife watched reality TV on. Dana had suggested he get someone to tend to his landscaping while consoling him about his premature ejaculation. He really did need taller hedges.

"We sold the house and bought one in Brentwood. I got a lawn guy that comes through every other week. I've also started exploring the avenue of male performance enhancement drugs."

Dana smiled as she picked up the last folder that Paul had tossed on the table. "Well, you should go hard for me next quarter. You don't want to disappoint the boss, right?"

She couldn't resist taking another stab at him. Reminding him once again how her proposal had led to her promotion to head up a yet to be named department. Lanno had played Darell off as a secretary leaving him with the task of getting her availability for next week so they could arrange to have lunch.

Dana was sure she'd be expected to be the perfect date and then screw the boss into a coma in order to secure her label budget. She smiled as she stuffed the last folder into the satchel.

"I'll see you around, Darell."

Dana lifted her satchel from the conference table and walked out the conference room. She left the conference room and handed her satchel to Skarz. She peeped at the wide checkered bangle watch by Burberry.

Dana had a meeting with Doug Jefferson from Tower records scheduled in an hour and a half at Four Seasons. She would convince him to give her the distribution she wanted now that she had solidified the financial backing and control over an entire division at the biggest record label in the States not to mention that her "niece" was the leading face in the hip-hop genre right now.

Dana sometimes laughed out loud when she saw a young girl with their hair dyed green and wearing jeans so tight they could cause a yeast infection. She had created and image for her protégé to characterize. Just like that, Annie was reborn in the form of a hip-hop sex kitten.

Annie was perfect for the role. She had dreamed of being a rapper all her life. Dana made her dream come true two years ago when she got Annie featured on Schemes debut album *Master Mind* with a song entitled *Make You Bust*. It was a Bonnie and Clyde cut with serious sexual references. Annie's verse on the song had established her as an artist.

Requests for her appearance to feature with other artist had become overwhelming. The world of hip-hop was full of fads so Dana acted quickly. She took her demo and portfolio to Roy Stevens, the label's C.E.O., and the same day they premiered the video for Make You Bust on MTV.

Roy was ecstatic over Annie's demo and eagerly approved the seven figure budget Dana had drawn up. Four million albums later, Dana had earned the credibility for finding talent she needed.

Scheme had sold eleven million records worldwide since his death, almost double what he had sold while he was alive. Dana needed to find another Scheme, and fast. It was almost time for Annie to get back into the studio and deliver another album. Without Scheme's witty lyrics and concepts, she wasn't sure Annie could live up to the hype she had created the first time.

Scheme had written or developed the concept for nearly every song on Annie's debut. On the eighteen track album, only two songs from her original demo appeared and neither of them were even considered for a single.

"Get me Cory on the phone," Dana said as she stepped back into the bedlam of the city. Her Rolls sat at the curb where she had left it.

Skarz handed her a phone and her satchel as she

ducked into the car.

"Hey, Cory, what you got for me?"

"Hey, Dana Dame," Cory responded, with a chuckle, "I got a kid you gotta hear. I'm running a session with him tonight. In fact I'm bringing him in on Annie's session. She actually wanted to meet him. Kid is sick."

Dana rolled her eyes. How many times had she heard that in the last five years?

"Yeah, how sick? Scheme sick?"

"Sicker. I'd been looking for this kid for almost two years. He was the one that shut the Castle down the night Scheme was supposed to perform there, on the eve of his murder. It was just chance that I ran into this cat. Remember the young producer we were looking at to do some production work on Annie's album? Well, it turns out he's the producer for a group called Hustle Kingz and this guy, Trey-Eight, is in the group. The kid, Fogg, is coming through tonight so we can record the WET track. I told him to bring dude through."

Trey Eight. Dana had heard the name before. She searched her memory and drew a blank.

"Okay, Cory, what time is the session? I might need to come through."

"Well, we are supposed to be recording five songs tonight. I told them to come through around nine. By that time, we should be halfway through the session. I met dude a few days ago. Dana, when I say sick, I'm talking terminally ill!"

"I'll be there and, Cory, don't tell anyone I'm coming through, not even Annie."

Dana ended the call without waiting for a response. She pressed her BlackBerry against her lips and looked out at the midtown traffic.

"Gordon, take me to the condo," Dana said to her chauffer.

Dana needed to grab her other briefcase with the lay out for her distribution plan for the next two quarters. Her ace in the hole was Scheme's highly anticipated sophomore album.

She had planned to release the first single, Whip, next Tuesday but, in light of her new position at the label, she may push the release date back until after her new position at the label is announced. She hoped this Trey Eight was all that Cory had hyped him up to be. She couldn't imagine a rapper better than Scheme. He had come into the game and set the standard for rap music in just a few short months with his stellar delivery and great storytelling skills.

His tongue was also lethal beneath the sheets but it was her tongue that had convinced him to sign away his publishing rights. Those rights had made her $2.7 million so far. She was expecting to make millions more once she released his new album.

Who would've thought the nappy headed, pigeon-toed girl from Bed-Stuy would be rolling like this? Not even she had given herself this much credit. But as huge as her credit line was it couldn't give her the one thing in the world she desired most, a baby.

G STREET CHRONICLES
A LITERARY POWERHOUSE
WWW.GSTREETCHRONICLES.COM

Chapter 3

Everyday Struggle

Trey poked his fork into the last piece of sausage on his plate and put it into his mouth.

"That was good, baby," he said pouring the last of the Promethazine from a cough syrup bottle into his Styrofoam cup.

Tina dabbed at her damp body and looked at the digital clock on her dresser. It was 9:47. She had an eleven thirty class. Tina watched Trey tilt the cup to his lips.

"When you gonna stop chasing your breakfast with that wacked out protein shake?" she said with an attitude.

"Why you always judging me? Let me do what I do! You don't understand."

She did understand. She had lost her mother in a car accident six years ago. It was crushing at first, but she struggled through her pain with no vices. Trey's mother was serving a forty-year sentence for drug trafficking and distribution. He rarely talked about her, but Tina knew they maintained close contact through letters. Trey hadn't seen his mother in the nine years since she was convicted. After her conviction, she was shipped off to Reno to a new federal facility for women called Beronica.

"I understand your pain. I just can't understand your weakness."

Trey shot up from his seat on the bed and tossed the Styrofoam cup and its contents against Tina's bedroom wall.

"You think I'm weak?" he shouted.

Trey grabbed his iPod and stormed out the room toward the front door. Tina caught up with him just as he started turning the locks to let himself out.

"Trey, I don't think you're weak! I just don't want anything to happen to you," she pleaded taking hold of his arm.

Trey pulled the door open and snatched his arm away from her. Before she could react, he was in the hallway and on his way down the stairs. The coolness of the hallway floor on the bottoms of Tina's bare feet reminded her that she was fresh out of the shower. She quickly stepped back into her apartment and headed back to her room.

She grabbed her cell phone to call him, but he didn't pick up. Frustrated, Tina tossed the phone onto her bed and slipped on her boy shorts. She sat on the bed to lotion her body. She rubbed her palm over the tattoo on her left breast that said Trey just as the first tear fell.

Tina looked at the picture of her mother stuck in the edges of the mirror on her dresser and she immediately pulled herself together. Tina's mother had never tolerated crying or whining. She would always say, 'Life happens. Can you continue on when it does?'

She touched a finger beneath her right eyelid and took a deep breath before getting up to clean the syrup off her wall.

Just as she was walking out the door of the apartment, Tina's cellphone rang.

"Hello."

"I'm . . ."

It was Trey but she couldn't hear him.

"Trey! Hello?" Tina said.

"Yeah, I'm here. A train was going by. I said I was sorry."

"No, you're not. You're the best rapper alive. Make sure you make them know that today!"

"I want you to be there."

"What?"

"You heard me. I want you to come through with me tonight. What time you get out of class?"

"My last class gets out at one fifty, but I have to come back to The Bronx to take care of something for my grandmother."

"Can you meet me on my block 'round six?"

"Yes."

"Okay, me and Boogs will wait for you. Don't be late."

"I won't, baby. I hate when we argue. I just know you can be so much better than the best that you know you are already. You know I love ya crazy ass right?"

"I love you more," he said before ending the call.

Tina smiled as she walked down 161st Street. She entered the train station and walked through the tunnel to the escalator that led up to the No. 4 train.

Tina had wanted to go to the meeting and session they were having with the A&R from Global. She had been their acting manager since she met them and Trey had convinced Boogs and Fogg that they needed her to manage their careers. She had done pretty well by them, too. She got them an ongoing paid slot at a club up in Mount Vernon once a month and the single deal she had gotten them at Precise Wax was a good opportunity, too.

She had even managed to get them some plugs with industry people through her course in school.

Her professor had gotten her some side work reviewing contracts for artist. The contracts were mostly for rock or alternative music groups but she had learned a lot about the recording industry's standard, and not so standard, contracts.

Tina was sure she could negotiate as well as any manager on salary. Trey normally asked her to come along with them whenever they were performing or recording a session, but since he had found out about Annie Oakley and the A&R he hadn't said a word about her coming, and she wasn't going to ask.

Trey calling back and apologizing made her love him even more. She smiled as her train pulled into the station.

Trey exited the train station at 116th Street and Eighth Avenue. The sun caught him in the eyes as he looked across the street at the crowd gathered in front of the chicken restaurant on the opposite corner. He squinted and then made his way toward the group.

Trey could hear someone rapping as he got closer. A few people noticed him.

"The king here!" a voice called out.

"I like my man ova whoever!" another voice said.

Trey recognized the voice as Bigga, a local dealer in the neighborhood. Bigga wrapped his arms around Trey and held him in a bear hug from behind.

"What's good, Bigga?" Trey said struggling to breathe.

"Niggas dun bought this cat uptown from Brooklyn talkin' bout he the hottest thing goin' wit dat spit," Bigga said finally releasing Trey and offering his palm.

Trey slapped his palm against Bigga's and smiled.

"I heard talk of bettin'" Trey said edging closer to the

center of the circle.

He noticed Maze, a hustler/ gangster/ rapper from 112th Street. He had his pick sticking out of his afro, as usual, but he didn't have the same cool look he normally had when he was competing. Trey was disappointed. The other rapper must've gotten under Maze's skin before Trey arrived.

The worst thing a rapper could do in a battle was lose confidence. The second worst thing a rapper could do was lose their cool. Trey eyed the kid across from where Maze and he stood.

"What's good, Maze?" he said brushing his shoulder against Maze's.

"Man, fuck this nigga, B! We don't fuck wit' dem Brooklyn cats anyway. Y'all a long way from home. Feel me?" Maze said looking at the rapper and his companions.

A chubby, brown-skinned dude who was standing with the Brooklyn crew threw his arms in the air and sucked his teeth.

"Yo, Bigga, what's good wit cha man? Niggas getting salty 'cause my dude is crazy wit' it. I tole you young 'un."

"Yo, Maze, fall back. Let Trey get dis nigga," Bigga said.

Maze twisted up his face in anger but he knew better than to challenge Bigga. Bigga loved rap and he liked Maze but he wouldn't be disrespected on his streets for anybody for any reason.

"Look, I invited y'all up to Harlem. You good, Fooquan. You know dat. Same as when I come through ya hood. Like I said though, I like my man ova anybody. Let's up the bet to five stacks," Bigga said as he pulled out the money.

"You want to put anotha' four stacks on this dude?" Fooquan said pointing at Trey.

He turned to his crew and laughed.

"I got one dude. Dis nigga got a label."

"You got da money, nigga?" Bigga responded.

"You know money ain't an issue, my dude. I love dat Harlem dollar. Let's get it!"

Bigga put an arm around Trey's shoulder and pulled him close and said, "Look, my nigga, dis for dat paper. Don't let me down!"

"What's my cut?"

"A stack and five ounces of syrup," Bigga smiled.

"Who goin' first?" Jarod said looking at Fooquan.

"You goin' first."

"Oh, hell naw. Dis my man house. Ya man goin' first!" Bigga said.

"Naw, Bigga, my dude went first wit' ya practice rapper," Fooquan said as he pointed a stiff finger at Maze.

"Man, fuck all dat," Trey said clearing his throat.

He stared the Brooklyn emcee down. He was a medium-sized, dark-skinned brother with nasty looking locks, definitely not the type you want to meet in a dark alley. Trey looked the rapper over as he ran through the readymade catalogue of lyrics he had in his head.

"Me and my niggas sling crack, bang rats in tha yard/ make witnesses change facts how we beatin' tha charge/ beat ya bones up wit' bats, ride you round in tha trunk/ wit my own shit full blast so they can't hear when you grunt/ shoot in a crunch, count shells as dey exit tha clip/ take out both ya knees shatter ya hip, clap at ya bitch..."

The crowd went wild. Their shouts drowned Trey's next four or five bars out. When he finished his verse, Brooklyn was all over it.

"I spit dis shit picture perfect no critique ta tha bars/ niggas be regular hood rap actin' like dey on Mars/ ain't nuthin' you could really see stars, I deliver wit' tha door open right from tha seat of my car/ spit it hard like all my life I been beefin' wit' cha'll..."

The two emcees were still going at each other a half hour later. The crowd had grown bigger and the tension was building with each round. The wager on the two rappers had climbed to ten thousand dollars. With that type of money on the line, it had become more than a friendly rap session.

"Yo it's on ya man, Foo. What's good?" Bigga said taunting Fooquan.

Trey had just spit a killer verse that left everybody stumped and amazed, including the Brooklyn emcee and his supporters.

Fooquan pushed the young emcee and said, "Yo, Anonymous, wut up?"

Anonymous extended his hand toward Trey and shook his head.

"You got it."

When Trey took his hand, the crowd went savage.

"Yo, Foo, you heard ya boy. I tole you my nigga, Trey, the best in the world! Yo, Johnny O, get my man, Trey, ten bottles of juice."

Bigga pulled a wad of bills from his pocket and began shuffling bills from one hand to the other.

"Yo, here Trey. Dis fifteen hundred and Johnny-O gonna take care of you on tha syrup."

Bigga headed toward a double parked gold Suburban that was where Fooquan was sitting with the passenger door open counting money.

Trey watched as Fooquan handed Bigga ten rubber banded stacks of money. Someone tapped him on his left shoulder. He turned around to see Johnny-O smiling at him with a cracked tooth.

"Hey, young blood, you did cha thang," Johnny-O said handing him a black plastic shopping bag.

Trey looked back at the Suburban before nodding to Johnny-O and heading around the corner. He walked down Eighth Avenue and took a left on 113th Street. The block was quiet. There never was much activity on his block. He waved to the group of old men who were sitting across the street from his building playing Dominos. That was a regular occurrence when the weather permitted.

Trey walked the five flights to the apartment he shared with his grandfather. He fished his key out of his pocket and let himself into the apartment. As soon as he entered, he smelled the remnants of fried pork. It was, most likely, bacon the one thing his grandfather seemed to have even when there was no other food in the house.

He headed to the living room to find his grandfather. Trey looked in the kitchen as he passed and saw that the sink was full of dishes. He shook his head and continued to the back.

"Pops," he said as he entered the living room.

Trey's grandfather barely grunted. He attempted to lift his head to look at him but his head was pulled back down by gravity bringing his chin to rest on the dirty tank top he wore. His pajama pants were just as filthy. Trey looked at the aged face that was surely going to become his one day if he reached his grandfather's age. The old man's salt and pepper afro was wild and unkempt.

He saw the glassine envelope with BIGGA stamped on it and the dregs of heroin in a folded matchbook. Cheering from the TV caused him to look at the Subway Series being played on the screen. Luis Castillo had just smacked one out the park giving the Mets a 4 -2 lead over the Yankees in the bottom of the seventh.

Trey shook his head before looking back at the coffee table where the matchbook was. He picked up the pile of mail from the table and sifted through it. He stopped at one envelope and dropped the rest of the envelopes back onto the table. He walked in his room and dumped the ten bottles of syrup on his bed. Trey picked up the Styrofoam cup from the small wooden stand at the head of his bed. He turned the cup up to his lips and sucked at the sweet syrupy leavings that crawled around the inside of the cup. He pulled open a drawer on and pulled out a pack of Jolly Ranchers.

Trey shook the hard candy into the cup, picked up the half bottle of Sprite from the stand top, and poured a third of it into the cup. He waved the cup around in his hand before setting the cup on the stand. Then, he poured two bottles of the syrup into the cup. He picked up a stained spoon and stirred the contents in the cup, and tilted it to his lips to take a swig. He sat down on top of the disheveled bed and took another swig of his lethal intoxicant.

Trey picked up the envelope he had taken from the pile, pinching it between the index finger and thumb of his right hand. He lifted the cup to his lips and read his mothers' name and the address of the prison in Reno for a few moments. Finally, he set the cup on the stand, tore the envelope open, pulled out a folded piece of line paper and started reading.

Jarod,

I hope my letter finds you well and in the best of health mentally as well as physically. As for myself, I am well. It was good to hear from you, as always. It is just sad that I hear your bitterness and disappointment in me even from the lines you write to me. I guess you are as talented with words as you keep telling me you are. I want nothing in life but for you to succeed. It seems that I should be the one that is bitter not because I am serving this sentence but because I am not there for my son. I pray for you every night from this hell hoping that you receive all of Gods' blessings. I believe in you more than you can ever know.

Thank you for finally sending me a picture. You didn't want me to see where they touched your pretty face. But you still my little handsome red nigga! And obviously the girls ain't worried. I see your little girlfriend. She cute. Nice figure, too. Be careful, my son. Beauty is poison. Fame is the dope that blinds true emotion. A person's values is determined by their heart. I love you always, my son. Release vices and embrace change.

Love always,
Mom

Trey put the letter back into the envelope and picked up his cup to take a swig. He looked at the picture of his mother and him in a bodega. It had been taken when he was around seven years old. His mother was wearing a grey sable coat with matching boots. She was smiling broadly and held her hands on her hips. Her four finger ring spelled out Redd, her street moniker, in script.

Everybody in Harlem knew pretty Redd. His mother had never talked about his father and he never thought to ask. When she was home she had met all his without complaint or request for assistance. He was definitely

Mama's baby. It was evident even in the photo. Trey was clinging to the fur hugging her leg.

Trey turned the cup up to his lips again and drained its contents. He felt so relaxed that he thought he heard the sports announcer on the TV but he couldn't be sure. He needed to write a new verse for the song they were supposed to record tonight. He made another cup of syrup, picked up his old notebook and a pen, and began to scribble.

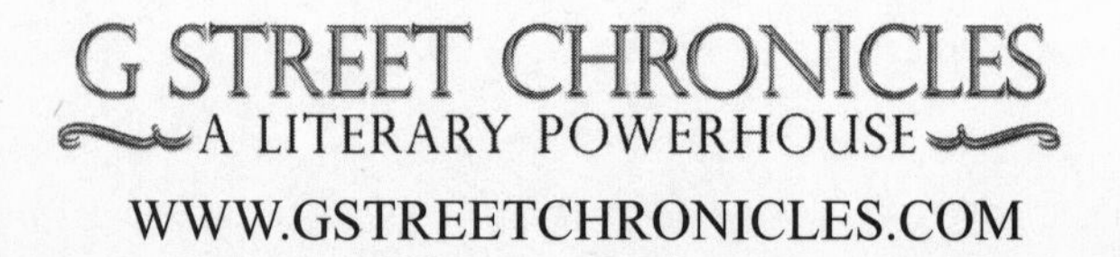
G STREET CHRONICLES
A LITERARY POWERHOUSE
WWW.GSTREETCHRONICLES.COM

CHAPTER 4

Stay Schemin'

The weather report predicted cooler weather in the city as the day progressed so Dana opted to change her attire after the meeting with Paul Lanno. She had taken a shower at the condo and changed to a grey wool pants suit by Chanel.

The suit jacket had a pointed collar, button front with huge gold-plated logo buttons. The shoulders were fully lined and there were logo buttons on each cuff. The jacket was four pocket design with the two breast pockets sewn shut. She rounded out the look with a gray Beverly Fieldman buck suede heeled anklet.

Dana decided to change vehicles, too, opting for the Porsche Panamera. It was an eighty thousand dollar gift she bought herself the week before when she received a check from one of the check cashing centers she owned out west. She loved the burgundy leather interior of the four door sedan. Porsche had really put this machine together. It was perfect for city driving. Dana maneuvered the gray sedan through the midafternoon traffic nodding her head to Bigga and Betta, the new single for Scheme's as yet to be titled sophomore album.

Skarz sat in the passenger seat staring at his Kindle. He occasionally lifted his head to look around and then he would go back to staring at the electronic reading device.

"What are you reading now?" Dana asked as she swerved to avoid hitting a Caravan.

"It's the autobiography on that kid from the show *Kings of Pavement, Quarters.*" Skarz said in his Barry White baritone.

"Oh, word! I watched that Monday night. Dude is doing his thing still. His girl, though, she the one. He got a book? What's the title?

"Yeah, it's called, *Change from a Different Dollar Bill.*"

"Right. Listen, I'm going to need for you to have your head out the books and reading this new cat we are supposed to be meeting at the studio. According to Cory, he's the answer to Scheme."

"Another Scheme, huhn?"

"A better Scheme," she corrected.

Skarz had been at her side for the last four years. He was an ex-MMA fighter from her old neighborhood in Brooklyn. He had suffered an injury that caused the MMA commission to disqualify him from the mandatory insurance needed to compete in the sport. The injury was only part of the reason he was disqualified. She had run into him back in the old neighborhood where he was a notorious stick-up kid.

Scheme and Dana had come out to show love for a block basketball tournament and to put on a performance. In the middle of Scheme's performance, a fight broke out and the crowd got out of control. Skarz had come to Scheme's and her rescue as they tried to get back to the Hummer limo they had arrived in. He had got them through the crowd with hard punches and kicks. Dana thought she had seen a gun as well but she couldn't swear to it in a court of law. When they reached the Hummer, Dana told Skarz to get in with them. He had been her personal body guard ever since.

Dana turned the Porsche onto the Brooklyn Bridge. Every time she crossed the bridge her chest tightened as she recalled the poverty she'd escaped. Her home in Jersey was a palace compared to the apartment she had grown up in on Gates Ave. Dana hated returning to the borough. Too many bad memories haunted her. She had told Cory he should move his studio into the city, but he didn't want to pay the price of real estate in the city.

Dana promised herself that she would look for a space for the studio in the city first thing in the morning. With her new position at the label, she could afford to splurge a little. She smiled as she thought about the meeting she had just wrapped up with Doug Jefferson from Tower records a few hours earlier. She had convinced him to sign a contract that would ensure the chain would purchase six million in new releases from her new label during the next quarter.

It didn't take much convincing. She didn't even have to mention her new role at the label. She simply pulled out the promo CD for Scheme's new album and it was a done deal. If Cory was right about his newest discovery, she'd be on the cover of Forbes next year. She pulled the Porsche in behind Cory's black Chrysler 300.

She wondered why Cory still owned the car. He was making good money working for the label. He could have been driving a Ferrari or a chauffeured Bentley. Dana loved being the center of attention. A Chrysler said normal. She was a star.

Dana got out of the car and headed to the studio. When she walked in, she saw a few guys and a girl in the lounge area of studio one. She walked into the studio where Cory was. Annie was in the booth and Cory was standing over the track board looking through the Plexiglas and bopping his head. Annie stopped speaking into the microphone when she saw Dana enter the studio.

"Auntie!" Annie said. She pulled the headphones off and walked out the booth to greet Dana.

"Hey, Keesh! How's the recording coming?" Dana asked embracing Annie.

She shrugged and said, "Okay, I guess. He's supposed to be writing the second verse."

Annie pointed at a dude wearing a black hooded sweatshirt and black baggy jeans in the lounge. The hood was pulled over his head and he sat on the couch holding a Styrofoam cup.

Dana looked at Cory.

"Is that him?"

Cory smiled and nodded. He headed toward the lounge.

"A, yo, Trey. C'mere. I got somebody I want you to meet."

The dude on the couch lifted himself up and tilted the cup to his lips before advancing toward Cory and Dana. A girl with a caramel complexion and a knockout figure walked alongside him.

"What's good, C? Who dis?"

"This, my boy, is the woman that can change your future…"

"Dana 'Delight' Peterson," Tina spoke up.

Dana looked at the girl with curiosity.

"And, who are you, young lady?" she asked.

"Tina Jones. I met you about two years ago at Scheme's album release party. I was with Crystal."

Dana stole a quick glance at Skarz at the mention of Crystal.

"Yes, it was a nice party. I'm sorry I don't remember you or your friend. Crystal, did you say her name was?"

"Yes, Crystal. She was with him when he was murdered."

Tina stared into Dana's eyes. She knew she was lying about remembering them from the party. She just didn't know why. The three of them had shared a table together all night ordering bottles of expensive grapes and pointing out the groupies in the room.

"Crystal. Wow. So, she was the girl that was with him when he was murdered. I think I may have met her earlier at the Castle that night. The crowd started acting up and Scheme never got to go on. I don't know who he left with. There were always girls around. I'm sorry to hear about your friend.

Dana turned her attention back to the dude with the hoody.

"So, I hear you are quite the spitter. Are you ready for your audition? As your friend here has stated, I am Dana Peterson, C.E.O. of World Domination Entertainment, the new hip hop division at Global Entertainment Group," she said as she extended her hand.

Trey titled the Styrofoam cup up to his lips and pulled the hood off his head revealing his face.

"I'm Trey-Eight and this is my partners, Boogs and Fogg."

Trey took her hand and was surprised at how soft her touch was. He could see her studying the scar on his cheek

"Cory tells me you may be looking to sign a new act and you need some material for the new Annie Oakley project."

She looked at Cory and shrugged. "That could be true, but I am not looking to sign someone I have to develop."

"You won't have to worry about development with them. They are the best," Tina said.

Dana turned her attention to Tina.

"Are you the manager or the girlfriend?" she asked with a crooked smile.

Tina returned the gesture and replied, "I am both, their manager and his girlfriend."

Tina grabbed Trey's arm as she spoke.

"Possessive. Okay, Trey!"

Dana clapped her hands together and laughed.

"Let me hear what you got. Go in the booth."

"Yo, Cory, pull up our track. C'mon, son," Trey said to Boogs.

Dana lifted her index finger and waved it back and forth at Boogs.

"I just want to hear him. Cory leave the track that's already pulled up, I want to hear him over that track. Wasn't you supposed to be preparing a verse for the song anyway?"

Boogs looked at Dana like she had slapped him in the face. Trey shrugged and stepped into the booth. He fitted the headphones to his head and adjusted the microphone.

"Yo go head and drop tha joint."

Cory went to the track board and pressed a button. Trey began bobbing his head. He blew a kiss at Tina right before he started speaking into the microphone.

"I'm from where Mc Donald napkins sit on top of toilets/ and the milks never in the fridge long enough to spoil it / Pops alcoholic moms insecure/ you hear pain from my jaws when I spit it at y'all/ I'm trying to add more worth to my signature… have the game in the figure four/ reingin' King like Scheme was/ a nigga from the hood that wanna rap/ the problem wit' that is the streets had a bigger buzz/ I grew selfish through ridicule, imagine pops never around and moms wantin' ta get rid of you/ fuck that gotta get dip school sellin' these bumps/ me and homie use to rap now I ain't seen him in months/ years passin' same shit, chasin' paper and blunts, acquiring most of my needs but none of my wants/ not thinking of a better plan, 'til one day I'm at this jam/ they play this joint, yo that's my fuckin' man!"

Dana looked over at Skarz as Trey flowed. He was bobbing his head, too, until he caught her eye. He knew what that look meant. They had found their next Scheme.

Annie couldn't control her excitement as she watched Trey's delivery in the booth.

"Yo dude is crazy. Are you recording this?" she asked looking at Cory.

Cory nodded looking at Dana for approval. The smile creasing her lips was all the confirmation he needed.

"Yeah, I'm getting all this. It's crazy."

When Trey stepped from the booth, he tilted the cup to his lips.

"I see you're impressed. It's nuthin'. I do this in my sleep."

Dana ignored the cocky rapper.

"Play the track back," she directed Cory.

He did as he was instructed and everyone listened again as the playback came through the speakers.

Dana turned to Annie, "Do you think you can imitate that same delivery?"

"Yes," Annie said excitedly.

"How would you like to be the author of Annie Oakley's

come back single?" Dana asked Trey.

"We'd have to draw up a contract so that his publishing is protected and the royalty rate is secured for a work for hire," Tina said before Trey could even respond.

Dana looked at Tina she knew this little *bitch* was going to be a problem.

"Of course, we will put everything in writing. You will be compensated. However, the company will retain all rights to the publishing. With an artist as big as Annie, it's standard. We can't afford to have her fan base jeopardized by revealing she has a ghostwriter."

"In that case, my client will need upfront payment for all songs he pens for this project. Since he won't be given credit for his writing through publishing, he will be selling it forfeiting all future royalty payments and performance rights. Correct?"

Dana rolled her eyes and said, "What business school do you attend, sweetie?"

"BMCC. That's neither here nor there. Annie's platinum status makes it impossible for us to accept anything less."

Dana watched Trey. He didn't seem interested in the exchange the women were having concerning his career. He just puffed his Newport and tilted his cup. He reminded her of Scheme, minus the nicotine habit.

"I'll have to recheck Annie's budget to see if we can afford that. We may need him to pen the whole album. Cory will be in touch."

"And, the track Fogg provided?" Tina questioned referring to the track Trey had just rhymed over.

"We'll take it, but we can only pay ten grand not the original fifteen you requested."

Tina looked at Fogg. He nodded.

"Okay, we can do that on the track, but Trey's verse can't appear unless we have a separate contract for his publishing for the amount I just stated."

Dana wanted to wrap her hands around the little *bitch's* neck. She had to get Trey alone to renegotiate just like she had done with Scheme. She had checked Tina out and the little wench was cute. And, Dana had to admire her fire. She had the same fire once. She knew if she didn't get this one under control it could start a real blaze.

"We'll have to see if Annie wants the verse," Dana said looking at Annie.

Annie nodded.

"I want the verse. I wanna push it as a single. Maybe we can bring him in on the album like we did Scheme."

"Yeah, maybe we could. I gotta see how this first single does. Then we can talk some more. In the meantime and in between time, I would love for you all to attend a party being thrown in my honor to announce my heading up Global's hip hop division."

"So, they are going to dedicate an entire department to hip hop or is it going to be the existing Urban Division that's being ran over there with a roster of acts that are placed in a specific genre of music because there's no department geared toward their specific music?" Tina asked.

"What do you mean?" Dana asked.

"I mean, for years, labels have been signing these hip hop artist and acts and they really have no idea on how to market them, mostly because they are just looking to cash in on what they perceive as a fad rather than a genre of music with staying power, such as pop or rock and roll. I mean if Global is going to really launch a Hip Hop Division there should be specific funds set aside for marketing the artist signed to that division and the artist shouldn't have to depend on an advance or loans from the label for marketing and promotion. Which usually eats away at the artist's budget and puts them in the red before the album is even released."

"Well, dear, I won't get into the specifics but artist will get promoted properly. We are not into failure over at World Domination."

Dana picked up the Hustle Kingz demo CD.

"I'll give this a listen to. Hustle Kingz might be our first act. Trey, Annie has a radio interview tomorrow over at MTV how would you like to come through and do a freestyle or sumthin'?

Trey tilted the Styrofoam and peeped inside the cup before turning it up to his lips.

"I could do dat. Wut time?" he said pulling a pack of Jolly Ranchers from his hoody pocket.

"I'll have a car pick you up tomorrow afternoon. Call me."

Dana nodded at Skarz who stepped forward offering Trey a business card.

He took the card and slipped it in the pocket of his jeans without looking at it. He seemed more interested in the empty cup he held. Dana and Skarz walked out of the studio leaving an excited Boogs, Fogg, and Cory behind. Tina was less than impressed with Dana and continuously pointed out the fact that Dana had intentionally lied about meeting her at Scheme's album release party.

Annie recorded three more tracks, two of which featured Trey and Boogs. Cory said he didn't know if the songs would make the cut for the album but he was definitely going to mix the tracks down and present them to Dana soon as he was done. Annie seemed confident that the tracks would make it onto her album.

Tina noticed how Annie seemed to be trying to stay up under Trey. Everywhere he moved she was on his heels. It was like he was the platinum selling artist, not her.

When they left the studio they all were hyped about the possibility of signing with Global. Tina didn't like Dana but she knew that getting them signed with Global could be the break they needed as artist.

She was determined to make sure that if Global signed the Hustle Kingz they would pay. Trey was worth seven figures alone. She wasn't going to let Dana get her claws into them so she could sell them off like some run of the mill rap group.

*****

When Trey and Tina got out of the cab in front of her grandmother's apartment building, the night air felt refreshing. He looked up at the clear, starless sky and inhaled deeply as she made a silent prayer. He pulled a blunt from his hoody and put a flame to the tip, the distinctive odor floated into the night.

Tina waved a hand in front of her face and twisted up her nose. She hated when he smoked Tarantulas, a combination of marijuana and syrup but she decided not to complain. He was in a good mood and she didn't want to disturb it especially after the argument they had earlier.

Tina was happy, too. She really thought things were going to work out for him this time, despite her feelings for Dana. She saw her reaction to Trey when he was delivering in the booth. She would definitely have to keep her eye on her.

Mrs. Daniels wasn't home. It was late. Tina figured she had stayed out at her boyfriends' house. They had the house to themselves. She went and started a bath and turned on the radio. Lil Mo's *4ever* came booming through the speakers. She inched up on him as he stood in the middle of her room.

She worked her body along with the rhythm of the music as she worked the hoody over his head. She turned him toward her and poked her finger in his bare chest and began to sing along with the song.

"Are you ready to be happy, Babe, for the rest of your life? 'Cause I wanna be your future...."

She stepped back and cradled her arms like she was holding a baby.

"'Cause I ain't goin' nowhere and you ain't goin' nowhere!"

She pressed a palm to her chest over her heart and pointed her index finger at Trey.

He smiled, "Who sing this?"

"Boy, you know that's Lil Mo'."

"You should let her handle the tunes. You a much better manager," he said stepping up and taking her in his arms as he laughed.

"Boy, please. I can blow."

"Riggght."

"Oh, shit, let me go stop this water," she said squirming away from his hold.

After they shared a bath, Tina rubbed him down with one of the scented body oils she had bought on the street from the vendors who sold the oils, incense, chew sticks, and other such items. She loved the smell of the different oils. She had over a hundred bottles. She dabbed some more oil in her palm and rubbed them together before massaging his back.

"I don't like Dana. I don't trust her.

"I didn't even realize she was the radio broad," he said lifting his head up.

"I don't know why that bitch lied about knowing Crystal. See, shit like that I can't stand. Don't try to play nobody off 'cause you moved from an apartment to a condo."

"Listen. Don't start making no waves over no bullshit! This could be it for us."

"Like I said, I don't trust her. Don't sign no paperwork with her until I look over it," she said putting pressure on his back as she massaged.

"A'ight, now. Don't be takin' that shit out on me."

"Don't give me a reason to."

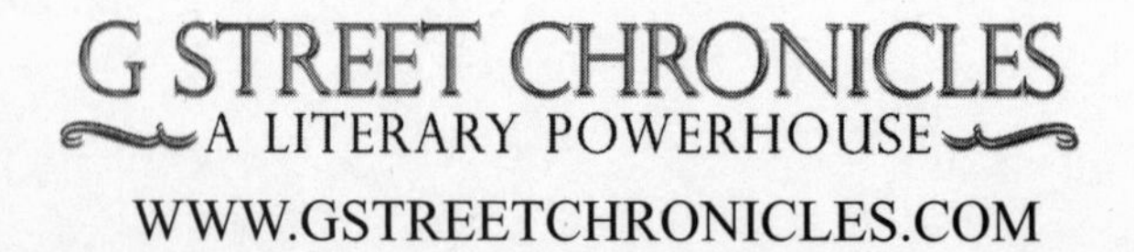
G STREET CHRONICLES
A LITERARY POWERHOUSE
WWW.GSTREETCHRONICLES.COM

Chapter 5

Just ta Get a Rep

Global had sprung for the Ambassador ballroom at the Plaza. The voguish styling and high ceilings were breathtaking. The lighting from the chandeliers created a warm and inviting atmosphere. Cristal flowed from elegant fountains and the help were all smiles and bow ties.

Tina poked a toothpick into one of the colossal shrimp on the seafood platter. Tonight had been magical for her thus far. She had met a lot of wonderful industry people and they had exchanged business cards. The highlight of the night was when her girlfriend, Camecca, introduced her to Kurt Strauss, the owner of A.B.J. He had a charming personality and, for a man in his seventies, he was really hip.

The real surprise came when she learned he was good friends with her finance professor, Mr. Cardona. Strauss promised to get her a paying internship at the company. She was elated.

Tina watched as Trey posed in pictures with Dana and Annie. Boogs had been chasing some R&B singer old enough to be his mother the entire night. It was funny to see him acting like a school boy with a crush. She would tease him about this one day as they sat in a room surrounded by plaques commemorating their accomplishments, she thought. This was the first official industry party any of them had attended and the guest list was sprinkled with star dust. She had met just about everyone she ever wanted to meet in the industry.

Tina popped the shrimp into her mouth and walked over to Trey. He had slipped away from Dana and her entourage of well-wishers. He was holed up in a corner with his cup. He was probably working out some song concept in his head while he was supposed to be having a good time.

"What's up, baby. You not enjoying yourself?"

Trey tipped the cup to his lips. He looked at Tina and smiled.

"I'm having a wonderful time. I'm just absorbing everything. Taking it all in. Dana got some real big plans for us. She talkin' bout sending us out on the road to do some shows with Annie. Then, she booked some time in the stu this week for us to go in and record some joints with Annie."

"Really? How much are you going to be getting for these shows?"

He cocked his head and looked at Tina.

"What? You my accountant now?"

"No, I'm the person you walked in here with. The person you sat up nights with and told your dreams to. The person that knows how hard you have worked and who has worked by your side trying to make it happen. Don't talk to me like I'm some chick you fucking."

"Look. I know you don't trust shortie. But, right now, she look like she doing her thing and I'm trying to ride this out and see where it's goin'. Ya dig?"

"All that is cute and shit. But if this thing you're waiting on to happen doesn't, we're gonna need some funds to make something pop on our own. So, when this ride comes to an end I'd like to have some gas money. Look around. Everybody is here smiling with her because she got that gwop right now. Come next year, if she's in the red, these same people will be ducking her calls and hiding the photos from tonight."

"I trust her."

"But you close your eyes next to me at night. Wake up, baby. That shit don't even sound right."

"Naw. It don't sound right to you because you always got some slick shit to say. Like your little college I.D. places you above a muthafucka. You and ya uppity ass grandmother judging me all the time like I'm some fuckin' deadbeat! You know? Sometimes I really be thinkin' you don't want me to make it. I think you scared if I make it I might leave you. You won't be in control anymore. Won't be able to criticize me for being a nigga wit' a dream. Scared I might find somebody else."

"Boy, please… The fact that you think it takes money for you to upgrade from the best thing in your life exposes your insecurities. It also lets me know you don't understand the value of what you have. Nothing my grandmother or anyone else says can change the way I feel about you. Only you can do that."

He reached for her wrist, but she snatched away quickly.

"No, Trey! For you to think that shows the question marks on your heart, not mine. Any money you ever make will be valued at nothing, once you add up the amount of time you'll spend wondering who I'm making happy. 'Cause I'm a good girl even for the wrong nigga."

Tina walked off. She wanted to get out of the ballroom

before the tears started. She was upset, but, more than that, she was hurt. She could feel the tears itching at her eyelids as she hurried toward the exit. As soon as she entered the lobby, the tears began to flow. A hotel employee approached her and asked if she was alright. She nodded and asked directions to the restroom.

She quickly moved to the sink to splash water on her face. She looked at her reflection in the mirror. She was truly happy for Trey. She hoped he got all he wanted and more from this life, the money, the fame, even another woman if he so desired. She could live with that. She could live with anything except to see him in Dana's arms.

Dana had seen Tina rush by looking like she was about to cry. She wondered what had happened. She had seen them talking in the corner a few moments earlier. Whatever had happened didn't seem to rub his little 'ghetto princess' the right way. Dana smiled to herself. Maybe her little scheme could work without the wrinkles of the girlfriend. Her mother had always said that if a man doesn't chase behind his woman, chances are he's looking under a different skirt. It was about time she adjusted her attire.

It was time to add a few logs to the fire that had been started. Dana walked to the microphone and tapped it to get everyone's attention.

"Good evening, everyone. Can I have everyone's attention for just a few moments? First, I'd like to invite Global's Chairman, Paul Lanno, to stand by my side as he has done so already by allowing me to launch this new venture. "

Paul Lanno joined her at the microphone forcing a smile. He really hated these events. He'd rather be in a hot tub with a half a dozen women ready to get down and dirty. Dana had been freaky beyond measure but he promised himself he wouldn't sleep with her again until she double their profit margin. He hadn't even wanted to see her again.

"Thank you, Mr. Lanno. First, I'd like to announce the first signee to the World Domination record label is none other than platinum selling recording artist, Annie Oakley!"

Dana started clapping her hands and the crowd followed her lead. She signaled for Skarz to bring her a box from the host table. Once Annie was at her side, she opened it and pulled out a thick link chain. The charm had been designed to look like some hands squeezing the globe and was covered with diamonds. She put the chain around Annie's neck and the crowd applauded again.

"Next, I would like to welcome Trey-Eight and Boogs, the Hustle Kingz, to the World Domination Artist Development Department of the label. We're hoping they will be our first multi-platinum selling group."

She pulled two more chains from the box. The chains were identical to the first one but they were smaller. Trey and Boogs came up to accept the chains. After Dana put the chains around their necks, they all posed for a picture.

"Don't worry. I'm gonna make sure your name is on that contract when they sign. You'll have enough money to buy your own jewelry," Tina whispered as she came up behind Fogg.

She had seen the look of disappointment on Fogg's face when he hadn't been called up as part of the group. She looked at the five of them standing together. Dana was all smiles as she pressed her body close to Trey's and the onlookers applauded.

Trey felt good. The chain around his neck meant something. It made it feel like the dream had come true already. Even though it was only an artist development situation right now, he knew what he planned to do. By this time next year, he planned on the Hustle Kingz and him being the top selling artist on World Domination and Global. He knew how to get the ball rolling.

He had noticed how Dana had been admiring his style whenever she came around which had been a lot lately. She tried to play hard with her smart business suits and thousand dollar shoes. He knew just how to play her too.

* * * * *

The next few months were stressful for both Trey and Tina. Dana kept him running around all the time. If he wasn't in the studio, they were doing shows. They had just come back from Detroit a few days ago.

Tina had been busy as well. Kevin Strauss kept his word and started her off with a paid internship at A.B.J. Two weeks into the internship her girlfriend, Camecca, and her partner fired their manager and hired her. She felt like she could do nothing but win with their platinum success previously in place. It was like she had arrived.

The hands-on experience she was receiving was priceless. She had learned so much in a short period of time. She was amazed at all the ins and outs of the industry. It was like she was wasting time in school because there was nothing in the text books about the real inner workings of these major companies. Still, she needed that degree for proper associations.

Tina missed Trey like crazy, but mostly at night or in the mornings. When she reached the condo they shared, she was dead tired and didn't even notice the bed was empty.

She wondered sometimes if he was laid up somewhere with a groupie, maybe someone who looked like the girls in the videos.

Tina got up from the bed and walked to the mirror in their bedroom. She looked at her reflection. Her body was tight. Her stomach didn't have a pouch. Her thighs were shapely and fit and didn't have an ounce of cellulite. Her skin was a smooth and soft. She put her hand on her hips and turned from side to side. She turned her back to the mirror and pushed her butt out looking at it over her shoulder. It sat perfectly in her sexy panties. There wasn't a dent nor dimple. *I* could be a video girl, she thought and giggled.

She walked to the small wet bar in the room and poured some pink Moscato over some ice, took a sip, and closed her eyes. She thought about her mother. She wondered if she would've been proud of her. She missed her mother, but she knew her life would have probably gone a completely different route had her mother not been killed.

Her sister and she had found a warm, loving, and caring environment when they had been sent to live with their grandmother. Life with their mother hadn't been cold, but it had definitely been nippy. Katrina, their mother, had definitely been the baddest bitch. Tina walked to the window and looked out at the landscape. She heard her mother's voice as clearly as if she was standing in the room with her. Don't ever go anywhere with a nigga without your own money and a way back home. Always make a nigga think he was getting some pussy. Never give a nigga some pussy on emotions alone. Love didn't build homes, money did. Never let a nigga bring you down. Always keep your appearance up it makes people view you as someone of importance. If you feel like you're giving too much of yourself to a nigga, *you* are!

She wanted to trust Trey, but she could tell something had changed between them. Their love making wasn't the same. It was missing that intense fire that used to be there. Now when they made love it felt like he was just going through the motions. A woman may not know every man, but she knew hers for sure.

She crawled into the bed taking her wine with her. She looked at the clock on the night stand on his side of the bed. It was 11:30. Trey was supposed to be performing in Brooklyn.

She exhaled. She knew where he was supposed to be, but she really didn't know for sure. Right now, he could be cuddled up telling her favorite jokes to a girl who had made it backstage. Only a man could make a woman feel like this. Stealing her confidence slowly until there was none left. Tina depended on him to fill her up. An incomplete woman was nothing more than a victim of a sorry man.

All of the decisions she had made since her mother had passed away floated around in her mind. She couldn't help but think she had failed in the worst way. She had fallen in love.

* * * * *

Trey draped a towel over his head as he walked off the stage. He felt like he was going to pass out. The club was jammed packed. He had performed here once before at an open mic competition, but that was before he had experienced opening up for Annie in front of twenty thousand. Now, doing the Zodiac seemed like rhyming on a street corner.

Boogs had been hyped about tonight's show for two reasons. The first reason was because they were performing a new joint they had recorded titled Body Snatchers. It was a diss track in response to Brooklyn rapper Anonymous. He had released a diss track going at them on Hatchet the Dee Jay's latest mixtape titled *Cracks in the Crown.*

The second reason Boogs was so excited was because they were performing the song in Brooklyn, right in his hometown. Epic! Brooklyn was known for its vicious reputation and to diss one of the residents in their own yard was definitely worth some stripes, far beyond the hip-hop world.

Boogs had brought like five of his homies from The Bronx with him and Trey had Bigga and about seven dudes from his crew show up. Fogg had an uncle that held a little weight in East New York and he came through with about fifteen guys from his projects. Trey didn't think it was that serious.

Before Anonymous had released the diss track he had been in street DVD's talking reckless about how his people and he were from the streets for real and how they had plans on exposing some fraud rappers in the city. All this started after he had seen them in videos opening up for Annie. They were on a platinum selling single and traveling the country. He was salty.

In one of the DVD's he had actually lied about the battle they had uptown. Bigga had just laughed when he saw the video with his man, Fooquan, standing next to this fraud co-signing him.

He'd said, "We know who spent the money. Foo is a funny dude."

When Bigga tried to reach out to Fooquan a few days before the show and got no response, they decided to mob up and head to the home of the coffin.

The crowd had been on ten the entire time they were on stage. Near the end of their set, Trey spotted Anonymous entering the club with a small entourage. They had performed the Body Snatchers track a second time and the crowd was even more amped than the first time.

Trey noticed how crowded it had become backstage, but he felt no cause for alarm. This was normal at these types of shows. Most the acts hung out backstage until it was time for them to go on or after they had finished so they could watch the next performers without the crowd boxing them in. Trey started seeing familiar faces the farther into the back he went. All he wanted to do was fill his cup and smoke a Tarantula. Boogs' homie, Smurf, approached him all smiles and gave him dap.

"Y'all murdered dat shit out dere."

"Word. All I need to do is take one to the head and go out there and try to find shortie with the red stretch pants."

Somebody bumped Trey from behind as Bigga and a few others approached him and Smurf. When he turned, he saw Anonymous standing with a group of dudes.

Anonymous took a step toward him. "What up wit' dat rap, homie? You know where you at?"

Trey pushed his palm against Anonymous' face so hard, it caused his neck to snap back, and threw his balance off. He saw Fooquan out of his periphery, but his movements were slow because of the syrup. By the time he had weaved what he thought was a punch, he felt the palm slap his chest and knew his chain was gone.

Boogs had come from out of nowhere and sucker punched one of the dudes standing with Anonymous. The dude's knees buckled and he fell to the floor. After that it seemed like an all-out brawl broke out and then there was a shot!

People started scrambling. Trey saw Smurf clutching a snub nosed .357 caliber pistol. He looked like he was about to take another shot before Bigga grabbed him and started pulling him toward the exit door.

Trey started following them. One of the dudes who had been with Anonymous was on the floor bleeding from the head. Trey scurried out of the exit with his friends and they all rushed toward their vehicles.

*****

"You know what you just won't listen. All you do is drink from that cup like it's going to make everything alright."

Tina was in his face. She was furious about the incident out in Brooklyn. She had been arguing with him since he had come in. He just sat there listening. He was tired of arguing with her.

"You keep fucking around. Do you know you could've been killed last night?"

He looked up.

"Ain't nobody gonna do shit to me."

"Oh, yeah. Well where's your chain tough guy? You running around acting like a gangster. That ain't what this shit is about. A mother woke up only to find out her son had been murder at a club over hip hop beef?"

"That nigga is dead because he was out there frontin'"

"Would you be able to look his mother in the face and tell her that?"

Trey waved his hand at her and answered his phone which had begun ringing.

"Yo, what's good, Dana? Yeah, I know. Some bullshit."

Trey got up from the couch and cut his eyes at Dana, as he started heading out the room.

"For real, Trey. You fucking serious right now?" Tina called after him.

He stopped in the hallway and turned to look at her. She could see the agitation in his eyes. But she didn't care. She hoped he seen the disappointment in hers. How could he take a phone call while they were talking, especially from that bitch?

"What you beefin' bout now shortie, huhn? I'm taking to many business calls. Somebody son gonna get shot?"

"You know what. I want you to keep doing whatever it is you're doing. I'm going out. I have a new client I gotta meet. Good luck with your business call."

Tina gathered her things and stormed out the condo they shared. A label perk that had come with the sixty grand the label had advanced Boogs and him for living expenses while they were in artist development. They had paid that back already with their show money.

Trey didn't bother to try and stop Tina. He was tired of her attitude. She was handling his business. He was about to handle his.

"Trey, you there?"

"Yeah, I'm here."

"Everything good?"

"Of course. What's up with this lawyer and the police that's supposed to be coming to see me?"

"It's nothing. Like I said, routine. They did the same thing when Scheme got murdered. A waste of tax dollars if you ask me. The hip hop police. They're never around when you need them. Like the regular police. Just let the lawyer handle everything. You'll be out of there in no time. Then, we can get something to eat."

"And, maybe a little more," Trey said.

"You gotta get your ifs, ands, and buts together before we can get to the maybes."

"I'll work on that."

"Yeah, do that," Dana said and then ended the call.

He thought about how Tina had stormed out. He was really starting to see who had his back, and who this business was really changing.

*****

Trey picked up the Styrofoam cup and drained its' contents. He had no idea how long he had been in his nod, but when he came out of it he heard banging at the condo door. He stood up and stretched. He picked up the empty cup and tipped it to his lips, his tongue licked around the rim of the cup for the drops of syrup.

He opened the door and was surprised to see two black men in their forties dressed liked they were on their way to a hip-hop concert. The tall brother pulled out a badge.

"Jarod Foster. I'm Detective Holmes. This is my partner, Detective Miller. We're from the Hip-Hop Crime Unit. We're going to need to take you in and try to get a statement from you concerning the incident last night. Do you know that boy died?"

"What boy?"

"I see we got ourselves a hardcore gangsta rapper. Okay, have it your way, Letterman. Lock up. Let's go," Miller said.

Trey got his keys and locked the condo before leaving with the two detectives. When he saw the Hummer they had to transport him in he almost laughed out loud. It was customized and could have been the main prop in a rap video.

The inside was a total surveillance unit. They had everything from cameras that recorded in all four directions, to fax machines and printers. The craziest thing was you wouldn't even know where the cameras were on the outside of the vehicle. He looked for them when they had got out at the precinct.

Before this, Trey had thought all the talk about hip-hop police was just rap. He couldn't believe there was an entire police unit dedicated to following rappers and trying to catch them committing crimes. He couldn't believe the amount of money being spent for cops to live the lives of entertainers vicariously.

They took him upstairs to their division office and sat him in an interrogation room. He had already informed them he was refusing to make any statement to them without his lawyer present.

The lawyer arrived at the precinct twenty minutes after they brought him in. He looked like a lawyer too, a Caucasian man in his mid to late fifties with graying hair. He was wearing an expensive suit and wired rimmed glasses He entered the interrogation room and pumped Trey's hand.

"I'm Johnathan Swartz. I was sent over by Dana. I guess she told you already. Well, what we have here is normal procedure. They just want to question you about the incident at the club last night. If you didn't see anything, you didn't see anything. Got it!"

His last statement was more of a directive, said with a stern look in his eyes, before he stepped toward the door and waved at the two detectives. A half hour later, they were still in the interrogation room and the detectives were still trying to find clever ways to word the same questions hoping for a different answer.

"Look. I tole you. I didn't see anything. My chain was snatched and a bunch of guys started fightin'. I got outta there."

Miller looked at the Jonathan then Trey.

"Look, kid. You want us to believe someone snatched your chain and you didn't pull out and bust a cap in his ass. Not buying it. We know how you gangsta rappers do it."

Jonathan cleared his throat and said, "Look detectives, my client has told you he knows nothing that can help further your investigation. He was a victim in this incident. If there's nothing else, I'm going to have to request you terminate this interview."

"Get him out of here. We'll be seeing you around rapper. Tell whoever in your entourage that fired that shot. We got more witnesses to interview and there's video footage too. You'll be back, rapper," Miller said.

Trey smirked as he left the interrogation room with his lawyer. He wondered if they really had video footage. If they did, they would know he didn't have a gun. That also would mean they would know that Smurf did. He had a feeling it wouldn't be the last time he would see the two detectives from the hip-hop task force.

G STREET CHRONICLES
A LITERARY POWERHOUSE
WWW.GSTREETCHRONICLES.COM

CHAPTER 6

Radio Suckas Never Play Me

Dana had set up some radio time for Annie and Trey as pre-promotion for the Summer Jam out in the Meadowlands. They were scheduled to be on 'The Geek's prime time spot the 5 P.M. traffic jam. The mid-town traffic was thick and they were running a little late. Trey made the chauffer stop so he could get a few pints of syrup before they left uptown. He had a lot on his mind as they idled in traffic.

Annie must have sensed it because she just toyed with her phone as she sat next to him. Her new album was getting great reviews and Trey was becoming a known figure cast in the starlet's light, an odd silhouette being that he was responsible for most of her hits. He sucked it up along with the checks. Tina and he had taken cruises and had travelled to South Beach four times since he'd been writing for Annie.

Tina had rented some office space in Queens and opened up her management company. She had gotten them invited to Bowie Adams' house one weekend. He was a legendary rock icon who was still making the charts after thirty years.

Trey couldn't believe all the concert memorabilia, plaques, pictures, and tour dates he had racked up over the years. He had an entire room dedicated to his career in music. It included Grammys and other awards and dedications to his music.

Tina was making headway with her managing business, too. She had used the invitation to Dana's announcement party to make all the right connections. She was quickly becoming a favorite at A.B.J. Her song choices and direction with their group BUTCH impressed the staff at the label, as well as Kurt Strauss. She was working on putting a package together for the Hustle Kingz and was trying to get them the budget she felt they deserved.

Dana was just keeping them idle at Global while Annie got all the glory. That artist development money and show money was garbage. They had the biggest buzz they had ever had right now, and they were featured on a platinum single. The checks had started rolling in but Dana was still playing games with some of the ghostwriting money Trey had coming. Tina just wanted him to just leave Global all together. She was confident she could get them a deal anywhere at this point.

Trey was starting to agree with her. The artist development thing was not where he wanted to be anymore. He was ready to go to the next level, especially after Tina had told him she had seen Anonymous up at the A.B.J. offices. He couldn't believe this dude was on the verge of getting a deal.

The police eventually caught up to Smurf for the shooting in Brooklyn. They did have the surveillance footage, but it was someone from Anonymous' camp who had ultimately identified Smurf. He was being held on Riker's Island on a million dollar bond. The label attorney had managed to get

Trey off with no charges from the incident but the hip-hop task force had a folder with his picture in it.

Fogg had started selling a lot of tracks to artist all over the industry. He was slowly becoming one of the most sought after producers in the business. Boogs had even been called in on a few projects from other artist. Tina wanted them to stop dealing with Dana, but she offered them a lot of opportunities even without a contract. It was hard for them to just walk away. The money they were making was crazy.

They were making great money from the shows they were doing with Annie. Some artists who were signed to majors weren't making the money they were getting from shows.

They were on fire right now. Trey was on three of every ten songs in rotation on the radio. He'd appeared as a presenter at the last BET awards ceremony alongside Annie and was included in the traditional hip-hop cipher and stole the show. It was time for something to happen.

Tina kept warning him to stay focused. Even though he was getting a lot of work now, and was running with Global, without a contract that could all come to an end, especially if he kept running around with Bigga and his crew. They had been traveling with him and Boogs everywhere they went. Trouble always followed.

Like the time they had traveled out to Detroit for a concert. Before the show they had an in store CD signing at Tower records and Maze assaulted a fan. Everything was going fine when they arrived at the mall, until two teens had recognized Trey.

"Yo, Trey, what up?"

One of the teens had yelled out and lifted his arms in the air.

"What's good, homie?"

Trey had responded back, and kept walking toward the store. He had started picking up his pace; as he started realizing more people were recognizing him. He was cool at shows in the comfort of a club or arena, but he didn't like when people approached him out in public. Had it been up to him they would've skipped out on the in store appearance; but Boogs wanted to do it. So he agreed.

"Yo. Trey!"

The same teen they had just seen were following behind them and he kept calling Trey's name. Then he started jumping up and down yelling '*The Hustle Kingz is in the building!'* By the time they had gotten on the escalator to go up to the second level. The teen was leading about fourteen to fifteen other teenagers following them.

When they got off the escalator the teen that had been leading the pack ran up on them with his phone. That is when things went horribly wrong.

Maze grabbed the kid's wrist with the phone in it and twisted as he swept his legs from under him. The teen hit the marble floor hard banging his head. Before Trey or Boogs could say or do anything. The other teens had surrounded them in a tight circle.

Maze started throwing haymakers while trying to dodge the assault coming at him. It seemed like punches were coming from everywhere. Trey had been hit twice before he started swinging back. Boogs was right on queue. Before they knew it they were in an all-out brawl with about twenty teens. It seemed like they were coming from all over.

The mall security had to call in the city police. The fight had sparked an all-out riot in the mall. Teens had started breaking in store windows looting and vandalizing. By the time it was all over Trey, Boogs, and Maze had been taken to the hospital and then to jail. They had missed the show; and they got hit with so many lawsuits. They could've opened an outfit store for every member in the Bar Association of America.

Global had spread some hush cash around and the lawsuits went away; and so did the news on MTV between commercials. After that they were right back out on the road. The label had to recoup all the money they had put out.

*****

Tina kept stressing to Trey that the image he was presenting wasn't a good one, especially with him not being signed to a deal yet. That could make majors shy away from him. These people in suits, don't want problems, they want dollars! She would always tell him. In their minds, anybody could be the next star. Hell, they'd make a star if the sky got too dark for them!

All these thoughts were running through his head as he rode alongside Annie in the back of the Benz on the way to the radio station. He knew The Geek was going to be grilling him about the Anonymous beef and firing a bunch of loaded questions at him. Dana had told him to keep the focus on Annie's single they were featured on and the success of the album. Trey had planned to take her advice, that is, until they pulled up in front of the radio station and he saw the cameras.

Annie jumped out the silver S500 and headed into the lobby of the radio station paying no mind to the paparazzi snapping shots of her. Trey got out behind her. He held his cup up for the cameras before taking a swig and heading toward the lobby.

"You'll get tired of it soon," she said.

Trey looked at the cameramen outside.

"Not as long as they want to be entertained. You gotta love it. It's show business."

"Yeah, but what about your privacy? I wanted to be a star since I was eight. Now that I am a star, I just want to be normal. I've been running through this fire since fourteen. I lost my virginity to a thirty-five year old producer on a recording studio floor. I think that's when I realized this was starting to become more of Dana's dream than mine."

He stepped on the elevator behind her. He wondered who the producer had been that had raped her. She had never said the words 'rape' or the name of the producer but when she told him about it, it almost sounded like she was reaching out. Did she consider it rape? At the time she probably thought she was being grown and sexy. She almost made it seem like her Dana had been pimping her out. The same thing Tina said she was doing to them.

Trey knew Annie really liked him. She always complimented him on how talented he was. She would call him sometimes and invite Tina and him out to her home. It was a six bedroom mansion in Amityville.

Tina had asked why she didn't live out in Jersey closer to Dana. Annie had said she really didn't like Jersey. Tina didn't like Jersey either. She also didn't like that Dana had tried to get them to move into Scheme's old house. It was just a bad situation between Tina and Dana.

The Geek was bobbing his head to the last leg of Middle Fingers Up by Annie, Boogs, and Trey. He was all smiles as they entered the studio. Annie grabbed her headphones and got comfortable on her stool. This was routine to her.

Trey looked around the studio at all the pictures and logos of artists on the wall, he had traveled all over the states had even been out the country once since running with Global but this was the first time he had been in the station with The Geek. He'd called in on a few phone interviews, but he'd never actually been in the studio.

There was a picture of a young Dana when she had worked at the station smiling with Capers, an old school rap duo who had helped pioneer street music as a sound and style. Trey had loved their early work. He took the headphones Annie was passing to him and sat on the stool next to her just as the song ended. The Geek dropped an atomic bomb sound effect before announcing Annie was in the building with Trey.

"So, Annie what's good? We here are again. You got the new album. You heating up the streets, the globe! And, you got company. It ain't Scheme but the chemistry is just as potent. Trey Eight! Boy, you sick! I'm feeling the mix tape *Phillies, Kangols, Nickel Bags, Sheepskins*. Interesting title. We gotta talk 'bout that later. So, the Queen is back, looking lovely as always. So, how this happen?" Geek waved his hand between Annie and Trey.

Trey nodded at Anne so she could set off the interview. He tilted his cup to his lips and continued to scan the photos on the wall.

"First of all, I want to say I got mad love for The Geek. I feel like you gave me my start in a way. You definitely broke a lot of big records for me and kept me relevant when I was out touring and these little Harlots were up hear stuntin' like they was the Queen. You know what it is. Annie Oakley is back! All these little hatin' bitches with they little YouTube videos and indirect songs on mix-tapes can fall back. The boss bitch is back in her throne.

After traveling the globe, gettin' paper and watching exotic sunsets."

Annie clapped her hands together and giggled.

"But, really I ain't even on it like that Geek I'm just trying to make good music for my fans. I wanna thank everybody that went out and bought the album. I definitely want to say thank you to my brother to my right. He is so talented. He really did his thang on the album. But the joints the Hustle Kingz been recording for their album are amazing. You know, I love Scheme, but I gotta be honest, I don't think I've heard anybody deliver like Trey," Annie said and looked over at Trey sincerely.

Trey looked back at her trying to read the honesty of her statement. She had switched right into artist mode the moment they had entered the studio. He had watched her turn on the charm so many times before blowing smoke up the rectums of promoters, radio personalities, even the executives over at Global. He was never really sure when she was being sincere. He knew she thought he was talented, but did she really think he was more talented than Scheme?

"Whoa that's deep! So, what you feel about that, Trey? You think you better than Scheme?"

"It really don't matter what I say. It's what the people say. I know I'm very unique and in that respect can say that no one really do it like I do. Some say I'm an amazing talent. What I say is I'm gifted. This is God. I'm just a vehicle to drive his will. That's why it's so perfect."

"So, look, I'm not gonna beat around the bush because I wanna know and the people definitely want to know. What's the situation with you and Anonymous? The reports about the incident backstage at the Zodiac are crazy! So, what's the deal? Y'all still beefin' or has there been some type of resolve? Because you and your camp have been pretty quiet since all this popped off."

"What you mean we been quiet? We killin' the charts right now! But, as far as beef, I can't beef with dude because I ain't seen him since the incident. I heard him talking 'bout the incident on different radio stations and all that, but no sighting as of yet. The funny thing and, what people don't know, is that this is the result of a battle that took place up in Harlem where his man lost like five stacks putting him against me. I guess he never got over it. C'mon, Geek. You saw the videos with him stuntin' wit' his man Fooquan. Then, he started saying little slick stuff on the mix-tapes. He called for me. I didn't want to disappoint so I responded giving him more of the same. Then, the shit went down in Brooklyn. His home town, I left without a scratch on me."

"Yeah, I saw the DVD where he was talking about the battle. No one really knew too much about it until he started speaking on it."

"Exactly! I dun push so many rappers face in the sand. I didn't even remember dude you feel me? Yo, my man won the stacks off dem niggas so we never addressed it. We actually laughed about it. I mean, to us, we lookin' at it as okay dis hip-hop. He see me and my peeps doin' our thing with Annie."

Trey paused and tilted the cup to his lips. He felt a surge of energy as the syrup eased down his throat and into his system. He was going to keep it professional once he seen how Annie was conducting herself. But Geek bringing up Anonymous and the syrup had sent him in another direction.

"Like I said, dude's a bitch. The real truth is that night in Brooklyn I put hands on that nigga. It's only so long you can talk shit before a nigga really see if it's studio."

He could really feel the syrup burning in his system. He could tell because his speech was broken and he wasn't putting his words together well like the wordsmith he was.

"There was a rumor going around that Anonymous or someone from his camp robbed somebody for a Global charm and chain."

"That's not a rumor, Geek. That happened the same night out in Brooklyn but Anonymous didn't snatch my chain. His man did."

"The kid who got shot?"

"Naw. His other man. The nigga know who I'm talkin' bout. What people don't understand, 'cause they watchin' these DVD's and shit of this nigga stuntin' like niggas chased us up outta Brooklyn. When shit ain't even happen like that. I got mad love for BK. But, Geek, c'mon. How can niggas say they chased us outta there and they man got shot and his other man is tellin' on my man? These labels is signing anythin' and puttin' gangsta on it."

He paused and tilted the cup to his lips again.

"So, you saw the person that snatched your chain. Did anything ever come outta that?"

"Anything like what? I definitely didn't file no police report identifying anybody. That's what I mean. These dumb ass niggas on the Internet showin' the chain and then showing a report the label made with the police for an insurance claim. Talkin' bout I'm tellin'. All dat shit is stupid. Tellin' on who? On what? My man in them cages. These niggas out here makin' YouTube videos. I don't know how they got that police report. They must be workin' wit' Detective Miller and Holmes from the Hip Hop Task Force."

Trey saw Annie look down at her phone. He guessed

it was Dana texting her telling her to take control of the interview. To hell with that! He was feeling hyped right now, not only about the situation with Anonymous, but with the Hustle Kingz situation with Global. They were one of the hottest acts in the country. Yet, they were sitting in artist development on one of the biggest labels in the business.

"You know he got signed to A.B.J. earlier this week?"

"Yeah, I know all about his deal."

"So, what's your situation? Are you signed with Global yet or are you still doing the artist development thing?"

He hated when he was asked about the artist development. It made him want to just walk away like Tina was suggesting but if he did there was no guarantee that the airwaves would still be open.

"Naw, I'm still doin' appearances and doin' my thang on stage openin' up for Annie. I mean Hustle Kingz is doin' our thang without a deal, but I'm sure something is coming soon. Our manager works hard I got complete faith in her as well as in the people over at World Domination."

He didn't want to throw Dana all the way under the bus but he had to let her know. He knew she respected a gangster. It was time he put some shade on the gentleman and came out with his other bag of tricks.

"That's right. You dating Tina Maxwell. Shout to Tina at Max Management. She's real down the earth. She was up here last week with BUTCH. She did mention you guys while they were up here. We had a real fun interview with them. Wow! That would be something if Hustle Kingz ended up at A.B.J. I mean I know your manager does a lot of work over there for them."

"Hey, whatever the situation we ready for it. On another note, look out for my appearance in BUTCH's new video for the joint Platinum Split."

"That's a hot joint. We been spinning it. I love your verses on the record straight crazy! So, when did you guys shoot the video?"

"We shot the video like three weeks ago out in Reno. Shout to the girls of BUTCH and all the people that worked to get me out to Reno for the shoot. It was crazy. I can't wait for the premiere so the people can see how we bringin' that real music back!"

"So Trey everybody wants to know what's up with the cup?"

"It's my personal cup! Whatever is in it just toast me when you see me. I'm sincere to whatever is in this cup because I always have it when you see me."

"There was an article written that mentioned you and your cup in USA Today. Did you see it?"

"Naw, I didn't. USA Today covered me and my cup? Hot."

He looked over at Anne and smiled. She smiled back at him with a hint of nervousness.

"Yeah, the journalist said with someone in your position you're sending the wrong message to the youth by walking around with this cup and rapping these vulgar lyrics. He went on to say hip hop music is becoming less and less relevant because of the content you are putting out. What do you say about that?"

"I say the journalist is a fool and the publisher is a bigger fool for printing it but I thank them both for printing about me in a paper as huge as USA Today. I mean the journalist says the music I'm making is irrelevant but he's sitting back talking about me and my cup in a national newspaper. Hip-hop bumped Country music from its' number one spot last year and made over a hundred sixty billion last year. Thank you for keeping me relevant.

"Hey, man, we are looking forward to it. I want to thank you and Annie for coming through. Miss Thang was real quiet tonight."

Annie laughed.

"Naw, Trey got it. I'm just letting my music do the talking. Besides, Trey is that dude right now. Watch out for him and I can't wait to be part of the Hustle Kingz project."

"Alright. Thanks for coming through and good luck in the Meadowlands I'll be there waiting for y'all to take the stage."

*****

Paul Lanno stopped the recorder and walked to the large picture window. He stuffed a hand into his trouser pocket and stirred the Scotch in the snifter with a twirl of his wrist. Dana had told him Trey had been in a situation but that it was under control. Based on that interview, it didn't sound like it was under control.

This is the room where Paul came to think when he was troubled. He called it the East Room in reference to the largest room in the White House by the same name. It was 2,500 square feet, half the size of its namesake. It was rumored that he had even paid Stephane Boudin the original decorator Jacquelin Kennedy had hired to design the original East Room. It was a divine replica. He cleared his throat getting his comrade's attention.

Gregory picked up his glass of Scotch from the table. He walked over to join Paul. The view looked out onto the golf course. Off in the distance, the green disappeared into thick woods. Sometimes, if the moon was in full blossom, one might see a deer or a coyote appear on the green at night.

Paul looked at Gregory and released a breath. He hated dealing with him. He was great at his job. It was his personal life that was a wreck. He was a pathetic pervert and he grew tired of covering up his messes.

The idiot had once sodomized the daughter of an executive secretary on a company camping trip. That had been a close one. Luckily, as usual greed over morals had fixed the situation.

As pathetic as Gregory was, he had an iron fist when it came to handling things for him. He had been behaving himself lately. Paul hadn't received a call in the wee hours of the morning with him on the other end saying he had strangled some stripper in quite some time.

"We have a few issues."

"Issues, sir?"

Gregory blinked his eyes and stared through the thick bi-focal lenses at the beady little eyes behind the glass.

"Yes, issues. Certainly, you didn't think I asked you over to play golf," he said stepping away from the window and taking his seat behind the cedar desk.

"I need you to keep an eye on the black bitch. Her and everyone around her. I think she's is stealing."

"What" Gregory said, looking dumbfounded.

"These niggers are out there playing mob with my money. I wanna know about everything their doing, especially her. Get a tan. Buy a fucking gold chain. I don't care what you do. I want to know every move they make."

The smile on Gregory's face appeared. He hated that perverted little grin but Paul had known that would be his reaction. Just the mention of stealing and, certainly a nigger, would get the rise he needed out of him. He didn't know if Dana had stolen a coin. If she had, Gregory would find out and, if she planned to, he'd stop her.

Paul's father had always taught him to think prevention. Murphy's Law wasn't squat as far as the old man was concerned. Anything could go wrong only if you let it by not foreseeing the problem.

It was his fathers' same adage that had made him come to the realization that he had to seize his inheritance when the old man decided he wanted to marry again. The geezer had found a new spirit with a Viagra prescription and a thirty-four year old blond waitress.

That's when Paul knew the old man was losing it. He had to take the reins before he lost everything. Gregory had been instrumental there as well.

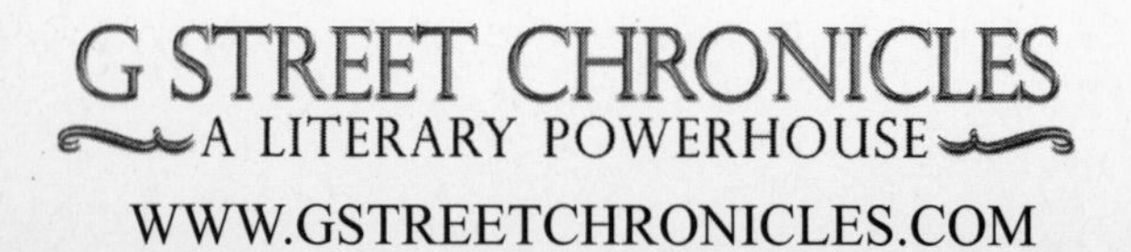
G STREET CHRONICLES
A LITERARY POWERHOUSE
WWW.GSTREETCHRONICLES.COM

CHAPTER 7

Under Cover Shortie

Trey picked up the magazine from the news stand. He smiled. There he was. His right leg was draped over the passenger door of the wine colored custom Aston Martin with the hard cover retractable top. He was sunk low in the seat with his Celtics fitted low on his forehead hiding his eyes in a shadow in the cameras lens. The Cuban link with the huge globe charm was playing second fiddle to his Styrofoam cup.

Annie was standing in the back seat directly behind Trey. She was wearing a fancy cowboy hat and a camouflage bikini. The gun belt around her waist had two thirty-eights stuffed in the holsters. Her pouty mouth and squinted eyes gave her a sexy allure that complimented all of her oiled up exposed flesh.

Boogs was standing off to Anne's left in a Lakers warm up suit. His fitted was pulled low on his forehead hiding his eyes from view. The tip of his cigar was glowing bright orange pinched between his fingers as he showed off his Rolex and a pinky ring.

The cover photo was from a photo shoot they had

done about three weeks ago for *The Hip Hop World.* The periodical was the hottest urban magazine on the newsstands and in mom and pop stores all over the united ghetto.

Trey had dreamed of being in their pages one day and here he was making his first appearance on the cover. He felt like his dreams were unfolding right before his eyes.

Tina was still making sure everything was in writing and the checks were getting cut but her focus had drifted to the other artist she had started working with. They were getting exposure and the show money was good but it wasn't a deal. His boo had come in the business and soared before he could ever get a proper take off and he couldn't lie. He felt a twinge of jealousy at times.

Trey knew Dana needed the Hustle Kingz more now than ever, not only to create a buzz for Annie's album, but also to help promote Scheme's. She had already had them appear in two videos for Scheme's sophomore follow up. They had decided to do the video for the exposure. They all knew Scheme's album was going to blow.

She was planning to release the videos in two weeks. No one had ever debuted two videos by the same artist on the same day. Trey had to admit she was smart.

He had decided to get his thug on with her for real though. The video shoot was the last time he had seen her and he had seen the look in her eyes that day. It was the look of seduction. Now, it was his turn to play hard to get.

Dana had started missing the money he knew she was making off them performing with Annie. But once they set the records straight with the label for the incident in Detroit. They started making their own moves. Their buzz had gotten bigger than it had ever been. Fogg was getting a lot of production from Global's other artists, too.

Boogs and he had started turning down the shows she had scheduled for them with Annie. They had started performing at venues Bigga had set up with dope boys in different cities across the states. They were the ones they had usually kicked it with when they were out on the road with Annie. The dope boys would treat them to bottles in VIP and put them on to the baddest females in their city. It was the best thing they could've done. The money was good and it was cash.

He knew he had her when she had called him early this morning and told him to meet her at the office by ten o'clock. When he arrived, she was in front of the building with a Bentley Azzure. Skarz was at the wheel. They had gone to a country club in Westchester for a private brunch where they discussed different rappers and producers.

He was actually surprised at how well she deciphered lyrics and styles. Under her hardcore business exterior was a passionate lover of the craft. She was no Tina but she had a passion for the music. It just didn't burn at the same temperature as her desire for money.

Dana had taken him to meet the promoters who were putting together the Summer Jam show in the Meadowlands. The promotion and radio people knew who he was soon as he walked in the room. It felt good butut it couldn't compare to the billboard sized posters they had hanging all around the stadium.

He was in the center between Annie and The Geek. Boogs wasn't on the poster but he knew Boogs wouldn't be tripping, they were a team.

Since that night when he had spit for her in the studio, it had been high end industry parties and constant work. If he wasn't in the studio writing for Annie, they were performing or recording their own material. He had cut all that off. Trey heard the desperation in her voice when she called.

"You like. Wait until you see the interview on the inside and some more photos from the shoot. I hope you like my choice for the cover," Dana said easing up behind him.

He loved the scent she was wearing. She had been throwing herself at him all day. His plan was working. He paid for the magazine and followed her back to the Azzure that was sitting at the curb. Skarz gave him a hard once over as he slid in behind her.

"So, where to now, lady?"

"Top of the world. If you're really ready."

"You know I'm ready. I'm not sitting next to you in the middle of the afternoon for no reason. You know I'm a star. I'm the complete package. You know you want me."

"Want you?"

"Yeah, like a desired effect."

"I've seen your type. You can't handle a woman like me."

"Handle… Ma, I was the star point guard for MLK. You'll be creaming with curiosity before I put it between ya legs and slam dunk. I don't do lay ups."

"Just a hard slam, no hanging on the rim, huhn?"

"Naw, I'm the type that like to get back on defense."

It amazed her how forward he was. Other than the cup she couldn't find a flaw in his character but she was sure one existed. Most the artists she came in contact with who came off as arrogant and cocky were masking their insecurities. She had seen multi-platinum artist break down during luncheons spilling their bedroom list in the search for a love that didn't exist. Some acted worse than the groupies that filled the concerts and music stores.

There was an artist on the Global roster right now

that had recently been indicted with a known heroin distributor. They had been stashing the dope and cash on her tour buses. The buses had built hydraulic lifts under the seats to hide the drugs and cash. They were supplying a major portion of the eastern coastline and most points in the Midwest until someone ran his mouth on the bus with some groupies. Next thing you know, something so perfect goes so wrong. A few of her people actually had got caught up in that sting.

Of course, Global bailed the artist out and was footing the bill for her legal defense. She had just dropped a new album that at the time that debuted at No. 1 on the billboard charts. They couldn't have her sitting in jail while people were demanding her presence all over the world. She had made them millions her last six times out.

Dana was perplexed by this cat that sat next to her though. He was different. Even the vice he carried around in the Styrofoam cup didn't knock his swagger off balance. He made people love it, embrace it.

"I'm the future. You know that, Dana."

"You know, in order for you to make millions, you gotta make me millions first. You know it's gonna get crazy once we set your budget up. I mean right now you're traveling on Annie's budget, but your budget ain't gonna stretch like hers just coming out the gate-"

"Why not? This ya thang? I been puttin' in the work," Trey said cutting her off.

"Yes, it is! This is my thang! But I worked for this. I believe in you. But that doesn't mean millions of others are going to feel the same way once we put a disc in the stores. On many levels, this culture is still a fad. We both admitted that earlier. All it takes is a cute dance song to come out in this genre and your whole project will sink and so will my credibility. You want a guaranteed deal with a solid backing. I want security. Boogs said he's ready to negotiate the publishing for this deal."

"I tole you, Dana. Tina handles all my and Boogs…" he paused to pick up his cup from the cup holder and tilted it to his lips, "… business concerning our publishing and all that. I tole you I just rhyme. Can we stop and get some Jolly Ranchers?"

She gave Skarz the signal to pull over at the next store. He pulled up to a Duane Reade as Trey's phone rang.

"Hello. Hold on, baby. Yo, listen, go to a store in the hood. I ain't paying for no Jolly Ranchers out this spot."

Dana jumped into action knowing Tina was probably on the other end of his line.

"C'mon on now, boo. You know I got you. Have you wanted for anything all day? Skarz, go get him some Jolly Ranchers. Do I need more candles for the condo?" she asked, "Grab some anyway. It looks like rain this evening."

"Naw, baby, I didn't forget. I know. I know. I'm down here in Midtown with Dana right now. I should be uptown within the next few hours. I love you, too."

Trey ended the call just as Skarz returned from the store with the candy.

Dana could tell from the conversation he had just had with her on the phone their relationship wasn't plagued by the usual insecurities you find between young people claiming to be in love. She'd have to create some insecurity.

"You have to get home?" she asked.

"Naw, Tina's managing this new act and she wants me to come through and do this verse I did for one of their joints. I guess they had an issue with the original producer. They got another track though. They just want me to do my vocals over. They're running a session tonight."

She cocked her head and gave him an inquisitive look, "Oh, really? Who's the group?"

"BUTCH. They're sort of an-"

"I know who they are, an all-girl alternative rap group, all lesbians, all femmes. Tina manages them?"

She was unable to hide her surprise. Global had been looking at them for some time. She even thought someone had met with them before. They were managed by Barry Ivine at the time and they couldn't get the deal done.

"Oh, yeah, she's been managing them for about a month. They signed with A.B.J. The lead singer, Camecca, is one of her homies from school."

The things you learn in the backseat of a car. So, Tina was managing an act signed to a major now? A.B.J. was really trying to make her earn her money this year. And, now, Trey was on one of their singles. If that single took off A.B.J. could be looking to sign the Hustle Kingz after all the work and money she had poured into them. She couldn't afford that she needed Trey to write for Annie.

Dana had been the hand fueling a beef with Trey and Anonymous. She had been hoping the beef would create pressure and make them anxious to sign, so anxious that they'd give away a huge portion of their rights. Now, he might end up on the label with his rival, and hers, too.

She thought about the Land Pirates situation and how quickly Mr. Lanno would snatch her budget if she dropped the ball. Dana doubted sex alone would break him away from his woman but she wanted to take a run at him anyway. If nothing else, it may give her some leverage over him.

"Skarz, stop by the penthouse."

The inside of Dana's penthouse was decorated in black and red. Even the onyx balcony had red lights in the ceiling fixture to highlight the night and cast a glow to the lights in the city's back drop. Trey was thoroughly impressed as he watched the afternoon turn to night. The syrup had him feeling real laid back and he had lost track of time. He vaguely remembered Skarz leaving Dana and him in the apartment.

He had rolled a Tarantula while he waited for Dana in the living room. She had gone to take a shower. He still heard the shower water running when he came out of his nod.

He looked out onto the balcony. Then, he checked his phone and saw he had three missed calls. They were all from Tina. He set the phone on the couch, got up, and walked onto the balcony. The night air was warm and the stars in the sky were few.

He thought about how his life had changed in the last few months. He wasn't signed to a major label, but he was making major moves in the industry and getting paid. He and Tina had just put the down payment on a house out on Long Island and they were both hot commodities in the industry right now.

Tina was putting together some of the best deals and managing some of the hottest talent in the game right now. The Hustle Kingz were running hard doing shows all over and creating a buzz.

Dana appeared behind him on the balcony. She stood nude in the evening light. Trey looked at her over his shoulder briefly and then returned to looking at the night sky.

"The night sky is beautiful. It's like a stage. All it takes is the right star to light it up," she said close to his ear.

"Stars fade with the night. I want to be the sun, the center of the solar system."

"It takes a lot to build that heat. I can introduce you to true fire though."

He turned to face her, "Torch me then, fire-starter."

"Show me your flame first," Dana said walking back into the penthouse toward the bedroom.

Her curves were enticing. Trey watched her backside sway from side to side as she walked. His heart surged with a sense of power at the thought of boning her and felt an erection formed in his jeans.

He entered the bedroom behind her and pushed her against a wall. She pressed her palms against the walls surface. Her legs were spread apart and she balanced her body on the front balls of her feet, with her toes were spread digging into the plush carpet.

He had her left buttock spread with his fingers and his tongue was teasing the opening to her anal passage while the middle finger of his right hand moved in a circular motion on her aroused clit. He could see her juices defeating gravity spreading all over her inner derriere, the moisture and wetness highlighted light hairs that would've never been seen had she not been so wet.

He squatted behind her on the tips of his toes, watching her reaction to his performance. On his right side was his cup, another part of his act, but that would come later in the show.

Dana bit down on her bottom lip and made passionate sounds of encouragement. He smiled as he continued to work her over. This was the casting couch in reverse and he planned to make sure she aced her audition.

He finally tasted her juices. The minute his hot tongue parted her lips and touched her insides she was set ablaze. She pressed her breasts harder against the wall and Trey smacked his palm across her ass.

"Where you think you going?" he asked taking her clit in his tongue and rolling it around raising her passion even further.

Dana smacked a palm against the wall.

"Fuck, you're good!"

"Better than Scheme?" he asked lifting his eyelids to watch her response as he dived back into her with his tongue.

"Sisssss...," she exhaled.

"Huhn, I can't hear you."

"Yessss, fuck yes!" She screamed.

This muthafucka was truly gifted, with his tongue. He was pretty sharp, too, but she was a true grinder. She sharpened tools to a true point of use.

"Ummm, let me see what the rest of you 'bout."

He stood erect and grabbed Dana around the waist and let his tongue run over her hard nipples. Dana leaned in and attempted to kiss him, but he turned his head. He released her waist and picked his cup up off the carpet and took a sip.

"I tole you. No kissing."

She felt a little embarrassed. She couldn't remember the last time she had been rejected.

"Nigga, are you serious? You just had ya whole tongue in me, licking my ass and all that! Now you talking 'bout no kissing!"

Trey took another sip from his cup and set it back on the carpet and walked to where he had left his jeans on the floor.

"Look, if you can't respect that, I had a nice time and I'm sure you did. So we'll call it even."

"You would really walk out of here?"

"Without ever lookin' back. The question is would you

really let me?"

Dana looked at the blood filled man meat that was pointing at her.

"Not without at least givin' you a try. It's like listening to that demo of the starving artist you ran into."

He smirked as he reached down for his jeans and removed a condom from the pocket.

"Naw, more like breaking a record you know is going to be a hit before the public ever hears it and you feeling proud to be a part of it."

He rolled the condom down his shaft and moved toward her. He smacked her on the buttocks. "Get up on the bed on ya knees and hug a pillow. Poke dat ass out. I heard Brooklyn girls like it deep."

"We do," she said while taking up the position on the mattress.

She felt him behind her. Then, he was pushing inside her, without warning and deep.

"Ahhh shitttt… yesss. Fuck!"

"I gets it in when push come to shove," he said holding her waist and starting a ride that turned into a full gallop.

Whenever she would try to pull away he would lift her up by her waistline and pull her to him grinding his tip into her stomach. Her words were lost in overwhelming breaths and her insides stung with ecstasy as her love hole released its cream.

The sweat at the small of her back glistened on her chocolate skin making it seem to melt away. Trey pressed his fingertips into her flesh as he felt his sac stir with his seeds. He was almost ready to sprout. His pace quickened and he knocked at her pussy walls with urgency.

She stretched out her arms and spread her fingers until they began to shake and the veins on the back of her hand looked like they were going to pop. He felt the final swell just before he shot his load into the tip of the condom.

He pulled himself free of her and headed to the bathroom. She lay on her stomach panting for a few seconds before rolling onto her back and calling to him.

"That was fuckin' intense! Where you goin', fire starter?"

"To cool down this log. I gotta get to the studio and lay my verse for the BUTCH joint. Shit was straight, shortie. We gotta do it again sometimes," he said over his shoulder before disappearing into the bathroom.

Dana lay there feeling her body starting to cool and her temperature starting to boil. *Had this nigga just played her off like some groupie after a concert! What the fuck!* Who did he think he was? She had made him!

Sure, he had put in a lot of work on Annie's album and it had met with great success but she had put him on the album. She'd put thousands in his pockets when there had been lint matching the dream in his head.

He had just dismissed her like she was the girl from up the block. Was he serious? She could destroy his career before it even started and the bitch he was running to wouldn't be able to do anything to repair the damage.

Dana had no idea Trey could be so pleasantly hard one minute and so disappointingly soft the next. Scheme had been begging to taste her honey hive. This worker Bee turned out to be a killer! She listened to the water run and began to rethink her scheme.

Chapter 8

Hating Love

"I told Trey and them not to sign this unless she changes this shit!" Tina said, holding up the contract from Dana that Trey had brought home the night before and shaking her head.

"What you complaining 'bout, now, girl?" Michell asked striking a pose in front of the full length mirror on the wall.

Michell had her hands on her hips. She was wearing an oversized pink shirt with a white outline of a cat printed on the front that hung off her left shoulder. Her black spandex pants were eye catching, especially with the hot pink lettering across the butt that read *PINK!* The pink and white wonder woman boots were designed to grab the attention of anyone who didn't notice her fine figure. She tucked the back of the shirt into the spandex, and winked at her reflection.

Tina looked at her sister like she was crazy. Michell never changed. She was always posing and making sure her sexy was turned up to the max.

"I'm talkin' bout this out of date broad, Dana Delight.

She already got Trey to take a hundred thousand for all his ghostwriting on the Annie Oakley album, twelve songs for a hundred grand! C'mon. She jerkin' him but he wanted to do the deal. Now, she wants the publishing from their album. Naw, fuck that!"

This broad had been trying to undermine her role from the beginning. She knew there was more money. Trey had mentioned Dana wanting to send them out West for a few months to appear with Annie for the last leg of her tour. He had already appeared with her in Germany a few weeks ago. That was big. Tina had to admit it. But this contract was garbage for all the work they had put in over there.

Tina planned to demand some amendments to the contract. Dana refused to include Fogg to the contract as a member of the group because he didn't rap. Bullshit! She was meeting with Dana, Roy Stevens, Huey Lincoln, and Paul Lanno at the Global office later this evening to do the paperwork. They better have a secretary working late, she thought, as she let the contract slip from her fingers onto the bed.

The more Tina thought about it, the more upset she became. Dana wouldn't be able to fool her with promises of cash on the backend and certain success like she had been doing to Trey and Boogs. It really infuriated her because she felt like this broad was using her man. Her mothers' words came to mind. *Never let another bitch fix your man's plate.*

She could get them a proper deal almost anywhere at this point. She planned to make that known at the meeting tonight, too. She wouldn't deny Global's introduction to the mass market was key and very much appreciated but it was time for her act to grow into the industry with a family. They shouldn't be just some fly by night act that other artist used to heighten their success.

Tina liked Annie. They had been to lunch a few times and they always socialized at industry parties when they saw one another. She knew Annie was more than grateful for the work the Hustle Kingz had put in to make her album a success. But business was business. Lunch at The Four Seasons was just a chance to catch up on gossip.

She really hadn't liked the gossip she had been hearing lately either. Annie had let slip that Dana had been sleeping with Scheme on the low and had become jealous when he had started sleeping with some groupie he had met named Crystal.

Michell stepped away from the mirror and looked at her sister sitting on the bed staring off into space. Something was troubling her and it had to do with Trey. Their mother always said that the *only thing that can distract a woman from taking over the world is a man!* She wondered what that fool, Trey, had done now.

Michell had flown in to go to the show in the Meadowlands Arena at the end of the week. She was so proud of her sister. She had begged Tina to move with her to Texas two years ago where she had received a full academic scholarship to Texas A&M. Tina instead stayed in New York promising to be some music mogul diva when she returned. She wasn't exactly a mogul yet, but she was, and always had been, a diva. She didn't like seeing her sister stressed. She loved Trey, but she loved her sister more than anything in the world. She was her shero. She was always the strong one and she never gave up.

Tina had always fought for her beliefs, even when they were kids. When they were younger, the girls from Concourse Village didn't like for them to cut through their complex on their way home from school. The other girls from their neighborhood would walk around the complex, but not Tina. She cut through every day until the girls got tired of fighting her and just started speaking to her and whoever she was with.

Michell loved Tina and Trey's house on Long Island. They had a private pool, a yard, and a two-car garage. . The neighborhood was nice and quiet, so much better than The Bronx. She couldn't imagine why Tina was talking about moving. They hadn't been there long. They were in a condo just six months ago.

"So, y'all really gonna move out this piece?" Michell asked looking around the room.

"Ummm, girl, yeah! Look at this four-bedroom up in Westchester County that I found. It's sitting on three acres. I want some land."

Tina rolled over into a sitting position and grabbed the Tri-State Home finder from her night stand. She flipped the pages until she came to the house she liked. She held the picture up tapping the page with her left index finger.

Michell took the circular and looked at the stucco home. "Damn! Four hundred! Girl, how y'all going to swing this? I thought you said him and Boogs' contract wasn't right? Shit! Then, you know you need other shit…"

"That's why I'm telling Trey not to sign the contract unless this ex-radio personality start broadcasting some real bread. But, we could still swing it, even without this deal. We already got like two hundred thousand in the bank between us. Plus, he's owed one more check for about fifty thousand. And, I got a few things going on myself," Tina said laughing.

"We could swing it. Drop, like, seventy-five down on the house and have around a twenty two hundred dollar a month mortgage. Once they drop the album, they will be out on the road getting that show money, what I like to call sho' money, girl, 'cause God knows that bitch can't get a dime of what they make from live performances."

"Yeah, but what if y'all don't do the deal?"

"Like I said, we don't need the deal."

"I keep hearing you say we. Is Trey on the same page? You can't be trying to build the Barbie Dream House with a toy nigga. I know y'all was happy when y'all ain't have shit, but things is changin'."

Michell looked around the room again at the shoes and designer bags.

"When things change, people change. Where's Trey at? I haven't seen him since I've been here. I just hope you ain't the only one feeling all mushy and shit."

"Trey loves me. He doesn't need to make anybody else feel that love because it's reserved for me. Don't judge me."

Michell looked at her sister. She wasn't going to argue with her. She was just going to be there for her.

"Well, how y'all got like two-hundred in the bank? All these numbers you throwing out there, paid shows and shit! And, you been splurgin' without ya girl?"

Tina laughed and said, "We bought some gifts for everybody. You'll get yours before you go back. We went away a few times, girl, shit! What chu been doin'?"

She reached out and slapped a palm across Michell's buttocks.

"Dun got all dat ass back there now."

Michell squatted and made her right buttock jump then the left one.

"It's that good country eatin', girl. I swear. Since I been out there it's like my appetite is crazy! What grandma said when she seen the pictures I sent you?"

"Shit! We both said you was down there fuckin' outta both draw legs. You know grandma start talking 'bout she ain't taking care a no granchillin'."

Tina laughed and then put on a serious face and poked her index figure against her cheek and began imitating her grandmothers voice,

"Ummm, she sure is got big. You think she still going ta school? I ain't takin' care no babies."

They both burst out laughter.

"Damn, grandma thought I had dropped out?" Michell laughed harder.

"Yup!"

"Oh, let me tell you girl…," Tina reached for the home catalogue and continued, "…how this broad tried to get us to move into Scheme's old house."

"What? The one they featured on Hip-Hop Homes?"

Tina gave her a sideways glance.

"Not at all. That shit was probably rented and not even in New Jersey. He had a home, or should I say, the label owns a home in Wayside, New Jersey."

"So, what happened?"

"I mean the house is nice and all. It is an eighteenth century, fourteen room estate equipped with tennis courts and indoor and outdoor pools but, a nigga will need three record deals to pay it off. Plus, I didn't like the fact that another rapper lived there. New deal. New life. New house."

"I feel you on that."

"The crazy shit is when Corey took us out to show us the house it still had some of this nigga's stuff in it. How about I seen a picture of me, Scheme, Crystal, and Miss C.E.O. that don't remember me! The crazy shit is in the picture I was wearing my gray hooded fox jacket and the bitch kept talking 'bout the coat all night! I showed Trey the picture and we just laughed. Phony ass broad."

"I use to always get mad when I use to see that bitch on TV or one of Scheme's videos. You know how you never met a person but you just don't like them. That's how I always felt about that bitch! I know she better not be with the bullshit if we see her at the show this weekend or I'm going to sponsor her ass on YouTube in knockout Queens, for real though."

Michell extended her hand for a high five.

"That broad don't want no problems, trust me. She is just walking round tryin' to be high maintenance while she walking next to that ugly ass bodyguard of hers."

Tina's phone rang. It was Trey. "What's up baby?"

"Yo, where you at?" Trey asked sounding excited.

"I'm home. Me and Michell about to meet y'all at the office. What's up?"

Tina sensed something wasn't right. She could hear Boogs and Dana in the background.

"Yo, we at *Forley's.* I just tried some snail for the first time," he snickered, "Dana just gave me and Boogs two Porsches. Yo, dem joints is crazy. I don't even know how to drive a-"

"Porsches! Oh, hells no. I'm about to renegotiate your contract at the meeting I'm not-"

"Ain't no meeting. We signed already. The Porsches were a signin' bonus. We all over here at *Forley's* celebrating."

Tina could feel her temperature rising. She could tell he was off on the syrup which only angered her more.

"What the fuck you mean y'all are all over there celebrating? How the fuck you going to sign the contract without me? Dana gave you and Boogs Porsches and you at *Forley's* celebrating? While you was over there playing fear factor with that bitch eatin' snails and shit, did it ever occur to you to call your manager, nigga? Ya fuckin' girl who made all this shit possible?"

Tears streamed down Tina's face. Michell stood in front of her mouthing "*What?*

"I hope you enjoyed your meal, nigga!" Tina tossed her phone on the bed and jumped up from the mattress before sitting back down just as suddenly as she had gotten up.

"What's wrong?" Michell said coming to sit beside her on the bed.

She touched her finger to a tear that had fallen on the collar of her buck suede shirt.

"I'm in love."

Michell held her sister while she cried. There was nothing else to do. There was no cure for love. Their mother had told them not to get afflicted with that sickness. It was a terrible disease. You didn't even know the symptoms. You just woke up sick one day.

*****

"What's good, homie?" Boogs asked Trey.

"Nuthin'. Tina trippin'."

"I tole you she was goin' to be hot, my dude. Did you tell her about the Porsches?"

"Yeah. She didn't even ask what color, fam."

"Damn! Maybe we should've waited."

"Waited for what? Nigga, just last year we was hopin' to be in a position like the one we in now. We just signed to a major, got some new cars, and about to get our hands on some stacks! I don't kno' bout you, but I don't got no regrets. This been one helluva ride and, to keep it real with you, I might be ready to switch vehicles anyway."

"What you mean, my nigga?"

"Just what I said, son. We young. Both of us."

"I know, nigga."

"I'm not talkin' bout me and you. I'm talkin' bout me and Tina. She doin' her thang right now, too, and I been thinkin' 'bout it for a minute. C'mon, son. How many times I told you we might need to seek new management?"

"That's new management, nigga. We talkin' bout ya girl here. Listen, nigga, I know you wanna be me, but you can't," Boogs joked but he looked at Trey seriously.

"Naw, my dude. It's not even bout being single so much either. I'm just growin'."

"Man, which one of these groupies you dun hit that got you talkin' crazy? We talkin' 'bout Tina, my dude. She was right here dreamin' with all us."

"You wanna know what groupie, for real?"

"Yeah, nigga, where you been hidin' her at? I gotta meet her."

"She right there," he said and pointed at Dana.

Boogs' eyes followed his index and then looked at him with a sly smile. He gave him some dap.

"Damn, son, you fuckin' the boss. I know the pussy crazy. You a fuckin' creep. You just tellin' me?"

"Nigga, this shit-"

Boogs had given him the eye. Skarz had eased up near them while they were talking. Boogs didn't like him. Something about him gave him the creeps.

"Yeah, I feel you, son. Yo, I'm goin' to go out here and take some pictures in front my joint."

Trey gave Boogs dap and tilted his Styrofoam cup to his lips. He noticed Skarz watching him. He didn't trust the bodyguard. He always seemed to be lurking around whenever Dana was out of sight.

He had been at a few of the shows they had performed at with Annie and he would hang around backstage pretending to be reading his Kindle. Trey knew he was there spying on them. He tilted the cup to his lips again before making eye contact with Skarz, nodding, and walking off.

After they left *Forley's*, they went to the penthouse of Global Entertainment Group President, Roy Stevens. The way Dana moved around the suite you would think it was hers. When they first arrived she walked Trey and Boogs from room to room, explaining the different art pieces and their worth all the while ridiculing Stevens for being an undercover homosexual.

Trey wandered back over to the bar where he was greeted by a cheerful white man with a bow tie. He declined the offers of spirits and looked at the bottom of his Styrofoam cup. He peeped at the Movado on his wrist and wondered what was taking Maze so long. He had sent them uptown in the Porsche a while ago to go get a few gallons of syrup.

Trey stepped away from the bar and walked out onto the terrace into the warm night air. The sounds of the city greeted him. He took in a deep breath and exhaled. He looked down at the street and saw Boogs posted up next to his Porsche while the photographer Dana had hired took photos of him. He pulled out his phone and looked at the screen. He wanted to call Tina back and apologize, but what could he do. What's done is done.

Trey had things that he needed to do. Tina was taking care of her family with the money she was making. Her grandmother was in a cozy brownstone on Columbus Avenue. She would be retiring from St. Luke's in a few months with a full pension. His grandfather refused to leave Harlem. He was still on the *horse*, riding high too, since Trey had been giving him rolls of money.

Trey needed to take care of his mom. He needed to send her some real money and to see about getting her out. Trey wanted to let her know he wasn't disappointed in her and that he hadn't become a disappointment. He wanted her to know he was a man.

The buildings and lights began to spin. He saw the face of his mother and grandfather in the bizarre spectrum. The ground felt soft beneath his feet, almost like it wasn't there. He heard screaming from down below. When he looked down, the spectrum disappeared and he realized he was no longer standing on the terrace.

Trey was hanging off the side of the terrace holding onto the railing. His fingers were slipping. Just when he was losing his grip, a pair of strong hands grabbed hold of his wrist and hoisted his body back over the railing. He looked up to see Skarz. Dana was next to him. He whispered something into her ear and left the two of them on the terrace.

"You have to stop fucking with the syrup, Trey," Dana said before she turned and went back inside.

Trey shook his head and walked back into the penthouse. As soon as he walked in, he saw Maze walk in with a few more of the homies. He must have brought some people back with him. Trey half-stumbled across the room. No one in seemed to notice. Most of the people in the penthouse were high on coke. He took Maze by the arm and led him to a secluded part of the room.

"Yo you got the syrup, B?"

"Hey, superstar, don't fly away on us yet. Are you alright?" Bigga asked stepping in close to Trey and Maze.

"Yeah, man, everything good. I'm good."

"You sure?" he asked again arching a brow.

"Yeah, son. I'm good."

"Okay," Bigga smacked him on the cheek and then cut his eyes at Maze.

"I got tha Motts, my boy! But, yo, I got a news flash."

After Bigga walked away, Trey quickly snatched the bag from Maze and headed to the bathroom.

"I'll be right back," he said over his shoulder.

Trey closed the bathroom door and opened the bag. There had to be at least thirty bottles of syrup in there. He remembered he didn't have his cup and took one of the cough syrup bottles out of the bag and screwed the top off. He tilted the bottle to his lips and let the syrupy liquid pour into his mouth.

The bottle was half empty before he came up for air. He wiped a hand across his lips and screwed the top back on the bottle. He grabbed the bag and went back out into the penthouse.

"Yo, who ready to see us kill this show?" Trey asked aloud to no one in particular.

Skarz approached him and draped an arm across his shoulders and began leading him across the room toward Dana who was posted up near the bar with The Geek.

"Hey, kid, you ready to be the best rapper alive?" The Geek asked when Skarz stopped Trey in front of them.

"Naw, I'm ready to be the best rapper in the history of rap."

The Geek looked at Trey. He let his eyes roam to the bag the young rapper held.

"Great answer, kid. Just remember, don't carry no vice with you in this business. They'll ruin you, for sure."

The Geek stepped away from the bar without waiting for a Trey to respond.

CHAPTER 9

She Dug My Rap. That's How We Got Close…

Annie walked into the studio and dropped her bag on the leather sofa. She was wearing a silk tracksuit and a crisp white tank top with no bra. Her areolas were the size of fifty cent pieces and her nipples pressed through the cotton. Her weave looked natural and her lips shined with gloss.

She pulled the shades from her face and smiled at Fogg. He was so cute. She had been trying to get him alone for months, but he always seemed to be busy. So, she decided to book some studio time and called him in for a session.

"What up, Annie?"

"Hey. How long you been here?"

"I just got here, like, ten minutes ago. The security opened up the studio for me."

"Oh, okay. I don't want to keep you waiting, superstar," she laughed.

"Who you?" he laughed.

She loved his laugh and the way the dimples formed in his cheeks when he smiled. He had smooth, light skin. What turned her on most was his red hair that he kept cut low with 360 waves.

"I see they finally put the pictures of Hustle Kingz up in the studio," Fogg said pointing at the picture of Trey and Boogs on the wall."

"Yeah, I'm hyped for them. My aunt ain't stupid. Grimy, yes. Stupid, no."

"I see. She bought this studio. This like the biggest joint I been in on the East coast. Ya aunt definitely keep her game face on."

Dana had bought a warehouse and had it constructed into sixteen state of the art studios. She charged time against all the artists' budgets. Artist from other labels used the studio, too. The four main studios were reserved for Global and World Domination artist. They were set up in an entirely different section of the building.

"I brought a few tracks. You got any idea what you want?"

"I know exactly what I want."

She pulled off the track jacket and set it on the couch next to her bag. She walked toward the track board where Fogg was sitting at the computer.

Fogg spun toward the computer screen as she approached and began punching keys on the keyboard. The studio filled with a melodic beat. He bopped his head to the beat.

Annie walked up behind him and leaned close to him pushing her chest against his back and blew a breath in his ear.

"I want somethin' a little harder than that."

Fogg was caught off guard by her forwardness. He secretly had a thing for her. Before they had even met her, he had lusted over her picture in magazines. She was definitely a bad chick. She had a stripper's body and a

Catholic schoolgirl's face. Now, here she was with her breasts pressed to his back breathing in his ear. He felt like a lucky groupie as a woody formed in his pants.

Fogg spun the chair around and looked into her lust-filled eyes. His palms start to sweat as he slid them beneath the cotton material of the tank top to touch her hot skin.

Annie caressed the nape of his neck with her hands moving up to his head. Her palms glided along the thick waves covering his scalp. His palm felt warm and moist on her skin. Her center was getting hot. She closed her eyes and let out a breath as he toyed with her nipples.

Fogg let his hands roam back to her waist and lifted her off her feet as he stood up from the chair. He kissed her slipping his tongue into her mouth. Her mouth was hot and her tongue was electric. Annie ran her nails along Fogg's back as she wrapped her legs around his waist.

He looked at her as their tongues wrestled. He couldn't believe this was happening. He had literally dreamed of this moment, not in a while, but he had. Now, it was happening. Annie's tongue tasted like cinnamon. She felt so soft in his arms.

Annie pulled away from him and stumbled backward wiping her mouth. She looked at him with fiery lust in her eyes before pulling the tank top over her head. Her C cups were full and round. She tugged at the sweatpants next sliding them down her legs and revealing her bare snatch.

He was already nude and standing at attention by the time she got the sweatpants off and slid her feet out her Nike running shoes. Annie admired Fogg's chiseled chest and arms. He looked like the first Chippendale's Redhead Anniversary Special.

She didn't want to wait any longer. She pushed him back onto the seat, straddled him, and eased herself onto his hard dick. She rode up and down on his shaft grinding her way to his stomach. She loved the feeling of him inside her. Annie sunk her teeth into her bottom lip and let out a moan.

Fogg held her at her rib cage as she bounced on his meat. Her juices dripped down and her wetness was louder than the squeaky spring on the chair. She dug her nails into his shoulders panting loudly and moaning his name. He thrust his hips upward bouncing his toes off the floor.

"Ooooh ahhh… Ooooh… It's coming, it's coming. Oooohhh, shit. I'm cummmmingggg…"

Annie released a waterfall into his lap. She lifted herself up on his shaft and sprinkled his legs as she shook with pleasure.

He couldn't believe it. She was a squirter! He didn't even give her a moment to catch her breath before he lifted her into the air. He cradled her in his arms while he drove his rod into her like a piston. He started turning in a circle as he pumped until he had made a full three sixty. She hung her head on his right shoulder and squeezed his neck in a vise like hold. He was tearing it up!

Gregory ran an index finger around the tight collar of the security guard shirt he wore. He watched as Annie and Fogg went at it like animals. He felt his upper lip beginning to get hot with moisture right before he reached down and unzipped his pants. He pulled out his stiff four inches and started stroking himself.

The boss wouldn't be interested in the bitch's niece fucking this guy but he was. He was interested in fucking the niece himself. He relieved himself and wiped his hand on his pants leg. He smiled and stole one last glance before he eased the door back shut.

Fogg felt the tip of his dick swell and his sac began to

stir. He felt her love come down again just as he shot all his energy into her. His knees buckled and he brought her down to the floor gently. His chest was sweaty and his breath short. Fogg stared into Annie's eyes.

"That shit was amazing."

He got up and went to get his shirt to wipe his face.

"It was but I think you can do better," she said smiling.

He wiped his face and looked at her. She had lifted her legs in the air and spread them wide. Her wet center looked sweet. He understood the term eye candy now. He balled the shirt up and tossed it to the side. Fogg felt like a kid in a candy store as blood filled his organ again.

*****

Dana lay in her bed thumbing through Hip-Hop Weekly when she saw a picture of Trey and Tina. It looked like the paparazzi had caught them off guard as they were leaving Jimmy's Café on 7th Avenue. The cameraman was brave. Wandering around Harlem at night with a camera could get you killed.

As usual, Trey was holding his cup. He wore a platinum herring bone with the iced-out thirty-eight caliber chamber charm. Tina's aqua blue designer dress was a long sleeved, shoulder less number. Dana had to admit she was wearing the hell out of it. Dana's eyebrows bent and she tightened her jaw when she saw the suede Gucci pumps matching the dress.

She was pissed because she had the same pair in her closet. She had to remember to return them as soon as possible. She wanted nothing that fraud broad had, except her man. She felt herself going to that place again, the place she had gone to with Scheme. She always fell for the bad guy and then he broke her heart. Scheme was about to move that groupie, Crystal, into the house Dana had set him up in.

Scheme had started playing her off for some little tramp from The Bronx after all she had done for him. He was nothing more than a starving emcee with some bomb ass head when she first met him outside the radio station. He was cute, though. She knew he was from Brooklyn right away. His entire swag said it.

Scheme was in Polo from head to toe. He came bopping up as she was walking out of the station. He had seen Bruce Lover, her co-host. She thought Bruce was going to break into a run. He was shook up because of the Brooklyn bad boy.

"How you, girlfriend? You Dana, right?"

She had looked at him suspiciously.

"Look, ma, you good. I'm just tryin' to give you this disc. Check me out, ma. I'm that guy. I live the Lo Life but I surfaced for you."

"A'ight. I'll check it out."

"Naw, ma, you don't understand. I'm it. Check ya boy out."

"Okay."

Dana took the disc home and listened to it. He was dope. She looked for him outside the radio station every day for the next month and a half but he never showed. She reached out to one of her people on the streets and they found out he ran with a crew called the Lo Lifes.

Her people had given him her message. He had replied he would only take a meeting with her in his Brownsville neighborhood. She didn't know it at the time but he was scared to come into the city because he had been in on a caper that had involved one hundred thousand dollars in diamonds. That was another mess Dana had fixed for him.

Dana couldn't tell anyone why it happened, but it did. One night after a studio session she took him back to her apartment. He had put it down! They continued their sexual relationship, creeping for months but then he started creeping. That hadn't bothered her. What bothered her was how he had started trying to handle her.

She had told him about the baby she was carrying, his baby. He had told her to get rid of it. He wasn't ready to have kids at the height of his career, the career she'd built for him. In the end, it didn't matter. She lost the baby.

Scheme hadn't shown any emotion when she told him. He had told her it was for the best. He hadn't even asked her if she was alright. That was when she knew he really didn't care. She had loved him. She had even asked him to marry her. He had turned her down flat. When he had started talking about leaving Global and signing with another company, Dana felt like he was trying to cut all ties with her. She wasn't going out like that. In her mind, his lack of love had stressed her out to the point that she had lost the baby and he had done it on purpose. He could turn some little project chick into Cinderella? She had smiled when she had got the autopsy results and found out that Crystal had been with child. Scheme was really planning on crossing her. Dana had put crosses on him first.

Now, here she was again. Trey and she had said they were going to keep their thing on a creep level, no attachments. That changed for Trey when he had started telling his girl that he was going on the road for shows that hadn't been booked. Dana knew she had crossed the line when she started paying him for shows that were never scheduled to take place to keep Tina off his ass.

Seeing them together in that picture infuriated her

because she knew Tina didn't pay for a minute of his time. Dana was going to have to turn it up. Her biological clock was ticking and she wanted another shot at a child.

Dana could tell Trey was feeling her. He had started talking about how he was getting tired of Tina handling things for Boogs and him. He was tired of her complaining about the decisions he made. If he could think about firing her, Dana could convince him to leave her.

Skarz shook his head when she had told him her feelings. He scolded her for being so foolish. She was supposed to be playing chess and here it was she was falling for a fool's mate. He understood though because he liked bad boys, too.

Dana hadn't been surprised when Skarz told her he was gay. She had figured it out long ago. He never had a female in his life. It was a no-brainer. They had both suffered at the hands of the adults who were supposed to love and protect them.

Dana had watched her mother sell her body to the drug dealers in the neighborhood. Then, she started making deals for the hard white rocks in exchange for Dana's young body as well. It happened twice before she had slit her mother's throat while she slept. Dana dialed 911 when she came home from school later that afternoon.

It amazed her how well she had played the role of the surprised daughter who came home from school and discovered her mother's body. She fingered one of the dealers who had raped her as the person she saw around her house when she had come home. He was tried, convicted, and sentenced to twenty years.

All those days of not eating, people running in and out all hours of the night, and her mother smoking up everything she could were over. She recalled all the hungry nights and praying she didn't die of hunger before she could make it to school for the free breakfast. Dana would never lose her hunger because of those days. She had to make her own way in this world. She lived on an iceberg but she kept falling into dysfunctional love in an attempt to melt the ice.

Dana looked at the picture of the couple again. She paid special attention to the scar on Treys' face. It matched the scar on her heart from never experiencing love. Skarz's had said it was impossible for people like them to love. He was wrong. She loved Trey. She knew he loved her, too, even if he didn't know it yet. He was distracted by his little ghetto princess. Men didn't really know how to love. They had to be taught. She'd teach him.

*****

Teresa half-staggered, half-walked around the building. She looked down the street to where warehouse workers were loading trucks. She thought about heading in that direction, but the sight of a police patrol car stopped her. She headed in the other direction cringing at the bite of the addiction that was chewing on her nerves. She had slipped so far into her crack-induced coma that she paid no attention to her appearance. The short black skirt she wore was stained with semen and her breasts lacked the support of a bra under her pink tank top. Her stockings had long runs in them and the flat shoes she wore hurt her feet as she walked. Teresa truly looked a mess. She had been wearing these clothes for days. Her jawline sagged and her wide eyes looked wild and bugged out in her face.

Teresa wandered aimlessly around the Hunts Point streets, hoping to catch the eye of a potential trick. A green Taurus braked along the main street and the Caucasian male driver of the vehicle looked totally out of place in this section of town. Teresa rushed to the passenger door motivated only by her need for the money to get the drugs her body craved.

Teresa opened the door of the vehicle and slipped into the passenger seat. The driver was a clean shaven, middle-aged man with sandy brown hair. He appeared to be well-built. He wore an olive green fatigue jacket, a khaki button down shirt, and beige trousers.

The man looked at Teresa nervously from behind the thick lenses of his glasses. Teresa feared he might be getting nervous and didn't want to blow the trick. She needed her fix bad this morning. Teresa smiled revealing the missing tooth in her mouth, which only made her look more repulsive.

"Hey, soldier. What's your name?" Teresa said giving the trick the most appealing smile she could muster.

"Gregory," he replied.

His eyes roamed over her from head to toe. Gregory didn't bother to hide his revulsion at her appearance. In her state, Teresa mistook his expression for one of desire. Gregory pulled away from the curb suddenly.

"Whoa, hold up now, sailor! We ain't discuss nothing yet," Teresa said.

She was already planning to over-charge the trick for any sex acts she performed. The white tricks always paid well. She needed to come up. *Please, Lord, don't let me blow this trick*, she prayed silently.

Gregory quickly hit the brakes bringing the car to a jerking stop causing a car behind him to stop quickly to avoid colliding with his rear bumper. The driver of the vehicle behind him leaned on his horn and spewed obscenities as he drove around the Taurus.

"I thought we'd discuss that when we got somewhere more private," Gregory said in a husky tone.

Teresa became apprehensive about the trick. She knew most of the white tricks didn't like doing anything around the neighborhoods where they picked up whores. Most feared being discovered by the police. The majority of them were businessmen with respectable family ties at the other end of their lives.

"The customer's always right but once you leave the store with the merchandise it's a sale and all sales are final."

Gregory nodded and started driving again. He drove to a desolate area in the back of the warehouses that had become an illegal garbage dump. He shut the car off and dropped his large hands into his lap.

"Well, is this private enough for ya?" Teresa asked.

Gregory sat still and quiet for a long moment, then he looked over at Teresa and said, "Is two hundred a fair deal?"

Teresa couldn't believe her luck. Her heart fluttered with greed. Her facial expression matched that of a poker champion who had just drawn two cards to complete a royal flush.

She replied, "Two hundred is a fair price for fair service. Now, for three hundred, I'll take you around the world, to the moon, and back."

Gregory smiled weakly, pulled out an expensive looking leather wallet, and removed three crisp one hundred dollar bills. Teresa grabbed the bills quickly and stuffed them into her left shoe.

"Well, let's go, stud," she said climbing over the seat.

Teresa quickly stripped out of her clothes. Gregory was still in the front seat looking at her in the rearview mirror. The stench of old sex and body odor overwhelm the car's interior.

"Get back here, honey. This thang don't work by itself," Teresa said with a laugh.

Gregory reached into the glove compartment and pulled out a blindfold.

"Put this on, please," he said offering the blindfold to Teresa over his shoulder.

Teresa took the blindfold and tried to smile seductively. "Don't want me to see what I'm getting, huhn?" she teased.

She knew the trick probably felt a little self-conscious about his size, especially since she was black. The age old rumor about white men and their small pricks wouldn't even be considered humor in the black community. It was just one of those stereotypical facts, like all black people loved fried chicken or bought things they knew they couldn't afford.

After Teresa fitted the blindfold over her eyes, Gregory told her he wanted her from the back. He opened his door and got out of the vehicle. Teresa got on her knees in the back seat and braced herself on the left rear door's arm rest. The weight of the car shifted as Gregory climbed into the rear seat. Teresa heard him fumbling with his belt. Just as she was about to make a wisecrack, her head was snapped backwards with brute force. The thick leather of a belt encircled her throat. Gregory forced the full weight of his body against her boxing her in against the door.

Teresa struggled as the belt quickly cut off her oxygen and drained her strength. She was going to die. In her final moments, she stopped struggling and thought about the last good hit she had.

Gregory dragged her lifeless body from the car and onto one of the mounds of rubble. He took out his phone to snap a picture of her. Then, he got back into the car, unzipped his pants, and released his now rock-hard pecker. He started stroking himself, as he savored the picture of Teresa and inhaled her foul scent which still lingered in the vehicle. He came quickly just as he always did after a kill.

Gregory straightened himself up, tossed the phone into the passenger seat, and started the car. His nerves were calm again. It was time to get back to work for Mr. Lanno. Lunch was over.

* * * * *

The pool looked inviting. Trey checked out all the flesh in the expensive bathing suits splashing around and having fun. He turned to admire the view from the 7,500 square feet Spanish style home Dana had recently purchased in Beverly Hills. He felt like he was dreaming. These are the things he had hoped for and he was really living it.

He thought about how far he was from Harlem as he inhaled the fresh air and looked in the distance at the smog hanging over L.A. He pulled out a Newport and pushed it between his lips. Just as the flame touched the tip of his cigarette, it was snatched from his mouth.

Dana tossed the cigarette to the ground and spun the toe of her Chanel heel on it. "I thought you told me you were going to quit smoking cigarettes?"

"I thought you told me if I make you millions. You would make me millions?"

"Sometimes a king acquires so much wealth he loses sight of it. Me by your side makes you a very rich man."

"A king only loses track of his wealth when his banker is living better than he is."

Dana smiled and looked out at the view and then back at Trey.

"Well, maybe you should consider locking down your key asset so when you spin the dial you know your best interest is safe."

Trey lifted his cup to his lips and looked at Dana as he took a swig of his syrup. He had her where he wanted her now. She was pressing.

"Maybe I should just switch bankers."

Dana smiled at him seductively.

"We both know you don't want to do that. I handle your deposits better than anyone. You've said it yourself."

She leaned in close him and nibbled his earlobe.

Her tongue touched his tragus as she whispered, "Once a man lets a woman play with his ass, he's pretty much all in whether he wants to admit it or not."

She stepped back, winked and left him standing there watching her walk off toward her other guest. The moisture from her tongue was still warm on his flesh.

Trey felt a tingle shoot up his spine as he thought about the night she had stuck her tongue in his ass. It had felt odd and amazing. He tilted his cup again and watched her as she posed for a picture with the Mayor of Beverly Hills.

"Hey, Trey."

Trey turned around to see who had called him. It was Dahlia, one of Tina's friends.

"What's good, butterscotch?" Trey said giving Dahlia a hug.

"There you go with the butterscotch shit."

Dahlia pointed an index finger at him and laughed. Dahlia moonlighted as a video chick. She had once told him about a rapper who had suggested she let him eat her out with an Altoid. On the night she had agreed to do it, they didn't have any of the powerful breath mints. They improvised with a piece of butterscotch candy. The candy got lost in her vagina. Trey had laughed until he was in tears.

"Hey, you told the story."

"True story, too. How you been?"

Trey took a swig from his cup, shrugged his shoulders, and smiled.

"I'm gravy, baby. I got it all smothered."

I see. Dahlia thought.

"How's my girl? Why she ain't out here living it up with you?"

"She chasing her dreams and I'm chasing mines."

Dahlia gave him a serious look.

"Dreams can feel like a lifetime but they really only last for up to twenty minutes. Most are shorter. It's good to dream but dreams don't come to your bed. They come to your head. When you wake up, your reality may be much better than the potential nightmare."

Trey looked at her for a long moment.

"Still, the philosophy major, huhn?"

"Yup, the videos is to pay for the education to get me behind the scenes where they really be counting the money."

"I can dig it. I'm trying to get in the counting room, too."

"Well, don't have a crooked smile. They'll trust you more."

"I try not to smile at all."

"That's not good. 'Cause I don't remember you smiling much in Harlem either. Don't move from one apartment to the next. Start thinking about real estate. You'll find yourself in a much more fitting neighborhood. I gotta go talk to Harold Williams about this new video I supposed to be in. It was good seeing you. Tell Tina I said hey. Take care."

"A'ight, butterscotch. Don't go experimenting with no candy."

"You either."

Trey watched her as she melted into the crowd. Then, he started looking for Dana. His sweet tooth needed some sugar.

CHAPTER 10

This Is Called the Show

Tina whipped the Porsche truck into the parking lot at the Meadowlands. She was fuming but she paused before exiting the SUV.

"You sure you don't want to talk about it?" Michell asked.

"I'm good. I told you I'm a woman 'bout my shit. I just want to look in this bitch face."

Tina had gotten a call from one of her artists. She had attended a pool party at a mansion Dana had just bought out in Beverly Hills. Trey and Dana seemed to be a couple, and there had been a lot of other industry people there.

Tina thanked her friend for the information and sat in stunned silence for half an hour. After she finished crying, she got herself together to handle the situation like the baddest bitch. She wasn't going to chase no man. No matter how much she loved him.

Michell and Tina got out of the SUV and headed toward the artist media entrance. The music grew louder as they moved beyond the security check point and into the arena. They had only walked a few yards before the two lead members from BUTCH greeted them. Michell couldn't believe how beautiful the girls were in person. They were cute in their videos but, in person, they were gorgeous.

"Hey, chick," one of the girls said as they walked up.

"Hey, Camecca, Fahkirah. This is my sister, Michell."

"Hey," the girls said in unison.

"How y'all doin'? Oh, my God! Y'all are so pretty!"

Both of the girls giggled.

"Thank you. I'm Fahkirah," the lighter of the two said extending her hand. "Nice to meet you, Michell."

"Hi. I'm Camecca.-"

"And, together we are…," Fahkirah broke in suddenly.

"BUTCH," The two hummingbirds said melodically.

Fahkirah put a hand over her mouth and laughed.

"I'm sorry. We been waiting for a chance to do that."

"Girl, these two are crazy just like you. Y'all gonna get along fine. Who's performing right now?"

"Some girl group," Camecca said.

"Oh," Tina responded with a smile.

Camecca was referring to Partial Print, a neo soul duo that was their current competition on radio and video. As far as sales were concerned, Butch had them beat by 1.5 million which was the reason they were performing in the early part of the show. Butch was scheduled to close the show. The other band members were also their production team. They were all musician' and they planned to do an hour and a half live performance. The promoters felt that was big enough to beat Annie out even with her hot new release. Hustle Kingz would go on right before Annie.

"Did you see…," Tina started.

"Your beau?" Fahkirah asked cutting Tina off.

"Sure did. Their entourage came in, like, ten minutes

before you. He came over and gave us a hug, but girlfriend walked by us like we were some groupies waiting backstage. That lady need prayer," Fahkirah said referring to Dana.

"Or, some healing hands to touch her," Tina said. "I'm about to go to their dressing room. I'll talk to y'all again before y'all go on. Y'all ready?"

"Of course," the girls said in unison.

Tina and Michell walked through the large hallway encountering artists, industry personal, security, and, of course, groupies. Tina introduced Michell to a few people but she was brief. She was intent on getting to that dressing room. She took a deep breath before pushing through the doors of the Hustle Kingz dressing room. She was happy to see their name on the door.

As soon as she entered the dressing room, Boogs jumped up. "I told you she was coming, son."

He walked up and gave Tina a hug. She was mad at him but he was still her brother. She saw Trey break away from Dana as she embraced Boogs. She also caught the look of disappointment in Dana's eyes when she saw her. That was the look that let her know she was definitely trying to net her man. Trey approached her with those same soft eyes he always had when he had done something wrong and wanted her to forgive him.

His eyes were a little harder to read because her heart was a blindfold. She wasn't sure if the apologetic look in his orbs were asking for forgiveness for making moves without her or because he had been making other moves behind her with Dana.

"Listen, baby. I know you upset but, look, everything gonna work out. We gonna go on this tour in like two months and I'm gonna get the money for the house you want," he said and held his arms open.

Tina fell into his waiting arms and all was forgiven. His look of happiness had diminished all her anger and also let her know he still loved her. As bad as she wanted to walk across the room and put the swizz beats on Dana, she promised herself she wouldn't mess up this night for Trey or herself. This was his dream. He had made it. Whether she agreed with the terms or not, it was his dream.

"We good. I love you, Trey."

"I love you, too. What's up, Chell?" he said pushing Michell's shoulder.

"You, big star. You made it. I'm proud of you. You gotta come to my college and do a show? Everybody down in Texas be gone off that *Pose for the Picture*," she said putting up her hands in the sign for the square.

"Well set it up. See if she can get it done," he said winking at her.

"We gonna get it done. I'm gonna talk to the events council when I get back."

"Hey. I see you made it," Dana said approaching the group.

Tina looked at Michell then at Dana.

"Of course, I'm here. Here to support my man and to collect my management fee. I talked to Sam in Finance. He said I should see you. So, I'm seeing you."

"Oh," Dana said, glancing over her shoulder to where a few security where standing with a few record executives. Skarz was standing alone in a corner watching the entire room.

"The label has appointed road management until they can get some. Your management, two different hats."

Tina cleared her throat before she spoke.

"I wear both hats. If you look at their management

contract, which you have on file at your office, I have a stipulation on page four that I will road manage all acts I manage for the first six months of any tour dates. I wear many hats. I'm a graduate at this game. My twenty percent management fee?"

"This is hardly the place for business. Why don't you stop by the office? I'll have Janice cut you a check."

"This is the exact place for business. I saw people counting money when I came in. Surely, you've received the money for the show. What Annie getting tonight? You got my little change in cash."

"So, you want to be paid in cash?" Dana said looking at Tina squarely.

"Business is business. You signed my act without even notifying me. It's really a breach because I am supposed to look over the contracts before anything is signed but since they seem so happy…," she continued looking at Trey, "with the deal you gave them, I'll overlook that little business oversight. And, yes, I'll take cash. Have Janice write a receipt. I'm sure she's in the building somewhere."

Before Dana could respond, Maze burst through the door with a wild look in his eyes.

"Yo, I just saw the dude who snatched the chain!" He said excitedly.

Before Tina or Dana could react, Trey, Boogs, Bigga, and several others ran out of the dressing room. Fogg was still standing there with everyone else. Tina was the first one to go after them. Just as she made it up the ramp to the back of the stage, she heard the music stop. The crowd had taken on a different tone as well. Five huge security guards nearly knocked her over heading toward the stage area.

By the time Tina and the rest who had followed her made

it to the stage entrance it was too late. They walked out on a scene made for UFC rather than a concert. Anonymous and his group were fighting with Trey and his people.

The security that tried to intervene looked like innocent victims until the state troopers and police made it to the stage. Tina and Dana looked at each other as the police made arrests. For once they both were thinking the same thing, The Hustle Kingz had *fucked up.*

CHAPTER 11

A Few N.Y. Niggas Did Her in the Park

Boogs was sitting in the passenger seat of his E Class Benz on his old block, 152nd street and Jackson Avenue. He had the door open and his leg hanging out. The platinum plate with the platinum spoon and fork lay awkward on his chest as he reclined in the seat. He had no worries about flossing so hard in the famished community where he had grown up. Even though the wolves were always out, he was good. The people had love for him here and he loved them.

Boogs sponsored the basketball tournaments, brought the food, and paid for the entertainment – the whole nine. He had donated money to help rebuild the community center. He gave away so much in this community that no one had a reason to take from him. He wanted them to be a part of his success so that the true dreamers could see the reality wasn't that far removed. He remembered how it was growing up in the projects. He was always dreaming of a way out.

The O. G.'s that had the hood when he was coming up still had it and they had said he was bulletproof. He always kept an ace in the hole though. Bigga always warned Trey and him that things weren't the same for them. They were celebrities now. There were some crazed people out there that would try to do them harm just to become famous. Others might do them harm because they would never expect it.

Boogs had moved out to Teaneck, New Jersey, but he was in the city almost every day when they weren't on the road. They were still doing shows under the table setting up their own dates with dope boy promoters in the south who paid in mattress money, money they couldn't tell the label or Uncle Sam about. It worked for them.

The label didn't have a clue. They thought artists were waiting around for them to put a tour together. A lot of artist were, especially with all the dope boys and stick up kids running around the behind the scenes of the industry nowadays. The industry executives weren't going to take a call from Joe Smoe in Atlanta saying he wanted to book the Hustle Kingz. The flaw in the industry is that it was insulated. The people in those big offices worked by mechanics. They only followed methods that have shown positive results in the past.

While the label was waiting to deal with the promoters, they knew to get tour dates open. The hustling artist connected with the hustlers who couldn't get through to the office. Just like that, they were getting $50K in cash and star treatment all the way. These situations had a downside as well. You had to be careful. A few artists had been set up. When they showed up to do a show they were robbed of all their jewels.

Boogs wasn't worried about that. Besides the fact that the South absolutely loved them, they always rolled deep. Bigga even had a system set up for when they were on the highway to make sure they weren't being followed. They always kept two vehicles trailing them so they could watch the traffic around them as they moved. If anything looked suspicious, they had eyes in the back of their heads and the element of surprise on their side. Bigga definitely knew his stuff. He handled all of their security and Dana paid him a nice check.

The one thing Boogs regretted was that Smurf wasn't by his side. He had blown trial and was sentenced to a quarter. Boogs sent him money and they talked on the phone on a regular. Still, he could hear the bitterness in Smurfs' voice even as he congratulated him on his success. He knew he wasn't bitter that he had made it. He was happy for him, but a man can only clap so loud when he's watching the show from behind a concrete curtain.

He knew the one thing that would bring him some comfort would be to take care of the dude from Anonymous' crew who had testified against him at trial. He promised him he would and he was about to make good on that promise. Boogs had gotten a line on the dude. He knew where he slept and where Anonymous and he hung out. He wanted to get the two of them together. The plan was already in motion.

It was time to end this thing with Anonymous and his crew for good. Since the incident at the Meadowlands, things had been pretty quiet. The labels ended up paying off a few lawsuits and threatened to charge any future suits against royalties. No one wanted to lose money but Boogs did want revenge.

One thing he had learned quickly about these industry circles was that the groupies were mostly the same. He had been sleeping with a stripper who knew Anonymous. She and her girls had done a few parties for them and, apparently, he and his crew were rude and disrespectful.

At that moment, the gears in Boogs' head started turning and, obviously, so had hers. She asked if he wanted to set him up. She knew they had drama and she was willing to help him if he helped her in return. They reached an agreement and it was on.

He let her believe he was just going to have them robbed. He wasn't sure if he could trust her to get down with a murder. The fear of getting caught might interfere with her greed. As long as he kept her greed out front of her, everything should work like a charm.

Boogs never forgot Bigga's words as he constructed his plan. He lived by the words because they protected his hand in a high-stakes poker hand. *A greedy person walks in the direction of the blind man. They never see an ending.* With that in mind, he fed the stripper money even on her off days.

The last time he had gotten a chance to see Smurf he had told him things would be handled soon. It was the first time in a long time he had seen a spark of life in his eyes. He was trying to get him out on appeal, too. That was going to be a long process. It seemed like his homie was just withering away in prison. Boogs did what he could to restore some hope in him. He wanted to let him know that he hadn't got rich and famous and abandoned him.

Maze returned to the Benz holding a bottle of Ciroc.

"Yo, this the biggest bottle they had in there."

"Yo, fuck it. It's all good, son. Crack that shit open. I need a drink while I ponder our next move."

Maze got in on the drivers' side and cracked open the bottle. He poured two cups and passed one to Boogs. He looked at the chain on his chest and felt the same twinge of jealousy he always felt when he was around Trey or him.

They were both shining to the fullest and, even though they were spreading love, it wasn't the same as having your own. He had been asking them to let him get on their album but they never got him in the studio.

The album had been recorded and handed in to the label. He hadn't been on so much as a skit. He wanted to be out there in the spotlight not the guy they pulled into the camera shot just before the flash blinked. He had been traveling with them to a lot of shows. He had even been on stage with them and done a verse or two. His main role had been security not the uniformed type, but the type that actually held things down.

"So, what's good on that situation?" Maze asked as he brought his cup to his lips and sipped.

"It's going down soon. Don't worry. You ready?"

"C'mon, son. I been wantin' to get at these niggas. Bigga been keepin' me on the leash. I'm still out here in these streets for real, for real. Y'all the rappers, remember."

"I hear you, my nigga."

Maze cut his eyes at Boogs as he took another sip of the Ciroc. Envy coursed through his veins as he watched how relaxed he was in the passengers' seat. He could pull the .45 from his waistline, blow his brains out right now, and run his pockets. He could take the chain, push him out the car, and drive off the block. If he did that, Bigga would have him killed. He was making money off of them. One thing he knew for sure is: you don't mess with Bigga's money.

He had asked Bigga about robbing Dana once. He was sure his little man and he could handle the bodyguard. Bigga had shut him down immediately. Bigga had told him that if he even thought about robbing anybody associated with Global or World Domination, he would kill his mother. He hadn't even raised his voice.

Bigga hadn't always been a major supplier in Harlem. His humble beginnings had started with a cool demeanor and a Saturday night special to fulfill the contracts he was given by the Dominican drug lords up on Broadway.

Maze suspected Bigga had something else going on besides setting up the shows with other dealers' in the South. All he knew is that Bigga had told him to take care of the Hustle Kingz and to not let anything happen to his investment. Maze found himself spending most of his days getting high, sexing groupies, or traveling. He practically lived with Boogs in his Jersey home. They had grown close over the times they spent together. Still, jealousy often reared its head.

"Well, tonight a long night off. What we gonna get into now? This sittin' on the block ain't it, son."

"I can dig it. I might have sumthin' nice for us to get into," Boogs said and smiled as he pulled out his phone.

He was hoping she would pick up and she did on the third ring.

"Hello."

He looked over at Maze, tapped him, and smiled.

"What up?" Bogg's said.

"What up with you. I thought you was coming back out here?"

"What you told me when I was leaving?"

"That you was full of shit."

"Naw. You told me to come back when I was ready to get it in for real."

"Oh, so you ready?"

"Yeah."

"Boy, bye."

"I'm 'bout to come out there now, but you gotta have

ya down for whatever suit on," he said.

"I had it on last time. You just wasn't ready."

"Well, I'm ready now."

"You know where to find me."

"I'm on my way. Me and my man," Boggs said and hung up before she could respond.

"Yo, son. Who was that?"

"You'll see. Come on."

Boogs pulled his leg into the car and tossed back the rest of the Ciroc in his cup. He made himself another drink. He wanted his energy level to be on ten when he got to her. She had worn him out last time. She was a beast.

"Where we going, son?"

"Long Island."

*****

Maze couldn't believe what was going on. Annie was sucking his dick and looking him right in the eyes as Boogs stood behind her pounding her pussy. He hadn't realized where they were when they had first pulled up to her house. When she opened the door, his heart rate increased. The whole way to her house, Boogs had been telling him how he had a for sure freak. He had no idea he had been talking about Annie.

She had been wearing a silk robe with nothing underneath when they arrived. It hadn't taken long for her to lose the garments and start prancing around in her birthday suit. She taunted them both with her lewd sexually driven conversation. Now, here they were.

She drew her lips upward four inches until the head of his *dick* was visible. She flicked her tongue around the tip and then worked her jaw muscles to suck his meat to the back of her mouth seeming to gobble him up. When she worked her way back up his swollen stem she grabbed the rod and pulled it from her mouth.

She shook the huge organ in her fist. A thin line of drool hung from her lips to the head of his shaft. She sucked her drool into her mouth and spit it back onto the head of the *dick* and stroked his trophy to a fine gloss.

She looked over her shoulders at Boogs chewing on her bottom lip. He grabbed her waist and began to really lay into her. She took his pounding like a big girl creaming and moaning as she went back to the task before her popping her mouth back onto Maze's shaft. She felt her juices run down her inner thighs at the thought of his Mandingo-sized *dick* in her ass.

Boogs gripped her waist tightly and thrust forward with his waist. He heard the air suffocating in her pussy every time his balls slapped against her vulva. He lifted his feet on top of the mattress. So that he squatted over her back as he pounded at her center. He heard the sound of air suffocating in her juices as he banged her insides.

Annie was definitely about that life. She hadn't even asked for a breather after the serious pounding Boogs had put on her. Her body was still on fire and she wanted more. Maze didn't disappoint. He put her on her back and pulled her close to the bed's edge so that her ass hung off the mattress. He pulled her legs straight up so that her Achilles' heels rested on his shoulder blades. He beat the head of his meat at the base of her snatch producing a moist smacking sound that seemed to arouse his member to swell bigger than it already was.

Annie gasped and let out a sharp squeal as he penetrated her. He forced his way into the tight wet spot spreading her wider than she had ever been. She slapped her palms against the mattress and exhaled before sucking in another deep breath. It took him a few tries but he finally got his shaft to glide in and out her fiery hole. Her breasts shook uncontrollably once he got his rhythm and started really tapping her ass. Her cries sounded distant as he closed his eyes and pumped into her.

Boogs watched them for a few minutes before he headed toward the shower. He'd had enough. He was glad he had brought Maze along and, from the looks of it, he might be the one to break the bitch. He was admitting defeat. *She could go for sure but could she last?* he thought as he stole one more glance at the pair.

Annie had surprised him when she squirted. He had stepped back and marveled at her juices all over his stomach and the bed sheets. She could tell she was his first squirter. She crawled to him on her knees and teased the tip of his organ with her tongue. He grabbed a fist full of her hair at the nape of neck and pushed her head further down on his dick causing her to make gagging noises as saliva ran down the sides of her mouth. He was blown away but she had one more surprise for him. She hoped she could stand it.

He worked the lube around her anal cavity popping one finger in and then two. He poked at her ass trying to loosen her up so he could at least get his head inside. They had tried using her natural juices and spit, but it wasn't happening. He was just too big. Annie closed her eyes and worked her hips so that she was grinding on his fingers. She hadn't been pounded in the ass in a while and she was extra tight. She felt his fingers come out her ass and began to rub her pussy before he made another attempt at her ass with his dick.

She had taken a deep breath and prepared, but she

couldn't have prepared. When he pushed, her rectum exploded in pain. She screamed and cried simultaneously. Her outburst caused Boogs to come back into the room to see what was going on.

He stood in the doorway and watched as Maze punished Annie for fifteen minutes straight. When he finally released her waist she collapsed to the bed whining in pain as she tried to catch her breath. Maze's whole body was covered with perspiration and there was shit on the front of both of his thighs. Boogs shook his head and started laughing.

"We should've recorded this shit. Y'all a mess," he said as he walked away chuckling.

Chapter 12

Hatin' Love

The entire ballroom was jammed packed. Written for Smiles was on the stage putting on one of his best performances. Trey had flown out to L.A. to see Dana. She had been spending a lot of time on the West Coast lately. She was trying to launch World Domination West.

"Hold the fuck up. Hold up! I know these bitches ain't just walk in here late. And, look at the tall bitch they got with them. Put the spotlight on them ho's, coming in my shit late."

The spotlight flashed on the three girls' trying to hustle to their seats.

"Ahun. What y'all bitches spent all ya money on them outfits and had to catch the bus here huhn? And look at the tall one. Usually, a guy see some tall glass of water they getting thirsty for an Amazon. Niggas look at her and start thinking Geoffrey from Toy R Us."

The girls finally made it to their seats as the crowd burst into laughter from Written's punch line. The tall girl was a good sport she stood back up and turned her backside toward the stage and smiled.

"Bitch so skinny her jeans only got one back pocket! I see you, baby, straight up and down pussy. Straight up and down..." Written waved his hand up and down.

More laughter as he started walking toward the other side of the stage.

"Look at this muthafucka right here, y'all. Put the spotlight on this nigga!"

Trey started laughing and waving his hands in front of his face. He could hear the audience starting to laugh before Written said another word. He even heard Dana giggling next to him. Written had told him he was going to get him back for not shouting him out on his CD. He had even brought it up again when Dana and he had run into him on their way into Caroline's. Now, here was standing on stage with an entire audience.

"Do y'all know who this muthafucka is, man?" Written took two steps closer to the edge of the stage as he pointed down at Trey.

"This eight grade dropout is a New York's top guy in rap, some say alive. Can y'all believe that shit?" Written stepped back and stretched out his arms.

The audience broke into laughter.

"Naw, I'm serious y'all. This is Trey-Eight. He's real a New York's own bad guy."

The crowd applauded.

Written waved his hand. "Cut that shit out! I'm happy the brother is accomplished. But let me tell you what I don't like. No matter how famous or rich a nigga is... and the nigga rich! And, just like you all, I was impressed when I first met him. The nigga had two Bentleys. This was before he blew up and shit. I was impressed... until I listened to the nigga CD and I ain't get one shout out!"

Written looked down at Trey and Dana and shook his

head. The crowd laughed. Trey laughed and wagged his finger at Written.

Written started to smile before he started walking toward the other side of the stage.

"But, you know what really impressed me about this brother for real? When I met his girl."

The crowd began laughing again as Written wiped his left palm over his face and then breathed a deep breath into the microphone. Written start back across the stage.

"Let me tell you something. When I met his girl," Written said in a whine, "when I met his girl…her name Dana, y'all. I wanted to start rappin' my damn self! I was like, can I get a deal? She asked me if I could rap."

He took a step back and twisted up his lips.

"I said 'Hells no, I can't rap. I'm trying to buy some pussy!'"

The crowd went crazy. The entire ballroom erupted. People started laughing, clapping and stomping their feet. Women were getting out of their seats and raising their fist. Dana's hand was pasted over her mouth as she laughed. When the crowd finally calmed down, Written looked at her and winked.

"You know I had to ask the nigga, 'How you bag such a fine bitch, dawg?' He said, 'I got her with the things that came outta my mouth.' I looked at him and said, 'So, you ate the pussy the first damn day, man?'"

The crowd went into hysterics again.

"I looked at that nigga, gave him dap, and said 'I don't blame ya, man.' My name is Written for Smiles. Thank you for coming out tonight. Please, make it home safe."

The crowd gave Written a standing ovation as he exited the stage.

*****

When they got back to the mansion, they made love. A few hours later, Trey awoke and found Dana watching *Casino.* It was one of his favorite movies. He reached into the ashtray and grabbed the Tarantula clip he had left there. He sparked the blunt and waved his hand at the smoke. Dana never really complained about his habits. Every once in a while she would tell him to ease up on the syrup, but lately she'd been going with the flow.

Tina was always on his case about the syrup or the moves he was making. Even after they had agreed to separate their business dealings, she still chastised him about things. She acted like she was so much better than him. She was always talking about what people were saying about him and his cup. He had heard it all before. No one understood that he had it all under control. The Hustle Kingz' album had been out for six months and was still in the top 5 on the charts. They had spent two months touring outside the U.S. and they were nominated for four Grammy's.

He loved Tina, but she got on his nerves with all the bickering. She had asked him point blank if he was sleeping with Dana before he boarded his flight to California. He lied. He didn't know why, but he did. He had told her about a few mishaps he had with a groupie or two but he couldn't bring himself to admit to her that he was boning Dana. He could see in her eyes that a confession would have crushed her. She had made it easy to confess his infidelities with the groupies but with Dana it was different. A woman would hold a dog on a leash until she caught him in heat with a bitch she didn't like.

"You said you had somethin' important to talk to me about. What's up?"

Trey was hoping she was about to offer him a CEO spot or something at World Domination West. Dana looked at him and smiled. He knew right away it had nothing to do with the industry.

"How long we been doing this?"

"Doin' what?" Trey asked as he reached for his cup.

"This. What we're doing. Creeping around like some teens."

"Well, you knew what it was when you signed up," he said irritated.

He had thought they had moved pass all that. She hadn't come at him about leaving Tina in a minute. He thought she got it. He had told her he loved her because he did but he wasn't ready to leave Tina. Even though she complained and got on Trey's nerves, he didn't know if he could take not having her in his life. No matter what, he was in love with Tina. She was in love with him, too. He wasn't ready to let that love go yet. It was selfish and it was wrong but it was what it was.

"You know, you're right. I think I've gotten all I needed from you for now concerning this relationship."

"So, what? Are you tryin' to say you breakin'-"

Trey caught himself.

"You want to end shit? 'Cause I'm good with that!"

"Good. I wouldn't want this coming to an end to interfere with our real business."

"Okay, cool. I'll be on the first flight out tomorrow."

He drained his cup, set it on the nightstand, and turned over to go to sleep.

"There is one other thing."

"What?" he asked not bothering to turn around.

She picked up an envelope from the nightstand on her side of the bed.

"I think you should read this."

Trey rolled over, snatched the envelope from her hand, and tore it open. He pulled the papers from the envelope and started reading. As he did, Dana got out of the bed and headed toward the bathroom.

She paused and said over her shoulder, "Kiss the wifey for me when you get back home."

He couldn't believe what he was reading. He jumped up from the bed.

"What the fuck is this?"

He heard the shower water running, but got no response. He knew she had heard him. He barged into the bathroom and snatched open the shower door, and pushed the papers toward her.

"What the fuck is this?" he demanded.

She looked at him and frowned.

"What does it look like? I'm pregnant."

Trey felt his temperature rising.

"Well, whose is it because we ain't been fuckin' like that."

"Haven't we?"

She turned off the water and stepped around him as she got out. She grabbed a towel and dabbed at her body as she walked back into the room. Trey was right on her heels waving the wet paperwork.

"I ain't goin' out like that."

He tossed the papers onto the floor, stormed over to the bed, and lay on his back staring at the ceiling.

"I know right. You went all in. Got that juice on you and tried to merc sumthin'. You the one who stopped putting baggies on. I am carrying your child."

"C'mon, ma. You know better than that shit you talkin'. I ain't even on it like dat. You know I already got my wifey. We can't have none of dat whut you talkin'."

She walked over to the bed and gently traced a finger along his hair line with a manicured nail tip.

"Talkin'. We both exchanged some words, nigga. You knew the dos and don'ts and so did I. You broke a promise to yourself. You said you would never get caught up on this thing of ours. I gave you what you wanted. I'm what I told you I was always, a tiger Panthera tigris. You had your chance to back out. You didn't."

She looked at the TV screen and said, "Oh, look, my favorite part."

Sharon Stone stood in a huge walk-in closet surrounded by designer names and Robert De Niro presented her with an assortment of jewels.

Tray understood all of her sly remarks lately. She wanted him to know she had accepted all his challenges. He had thrown down the gauntlet when he told her his home situation was perfect and nothing could disturb that. Her sharp response had flowed smoothly, *'I'm a lethal combination of intellect, beauty, and bomb pussy. If you got that at home, don't leave home without it.'*

He had to admit he really was sprung on jones. She was exciting to him in many ways that didn't compare to the excitement he got from Tina. He loved Tina's personality. She was loving, sweet, caring, and strong. Her outer beauty was unique and made her strikingly gorgeous but she wasn't lively like Dana.

Dana was more energetic. Her beauty combined with her well-developed personality made her a show stopper. He had definitely been enjoying life under her big top until the clowns came out. How could he have played himself like this? All he could hope for is that he hadn't gotten his executive producer pregnant. If he had it would kill Tina...

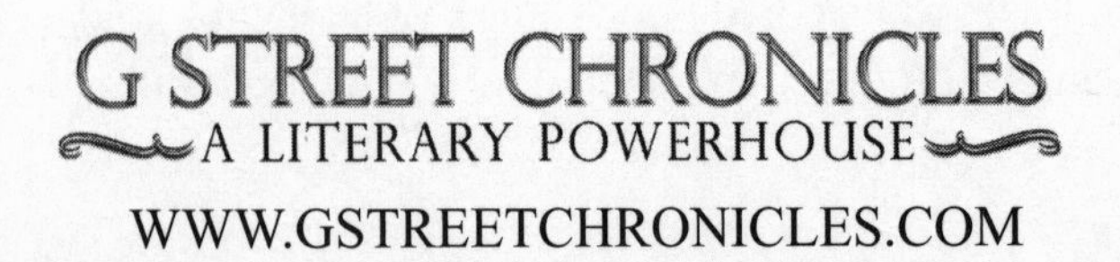
G STREET CHRONICLES
A LITERARY POWERHOUSE
WWW.GSTREETCHRONICLES.COM

Chapter 13

She Keep On Passin' Me By

Cory navigated his Land Cruiser through the heavy traffic. He couldn't help but to keep looking over at his passenger. Annie was looking down at her cellphone, blowing bubbles as she chewed, and bopping her head to the beat of BUTCH's new single Air It Out. As always, she was ignoring him. Her eyes were hidden behind her designer shades.

They were on their way to Toronto where she would be headlining a concert and doing an in-store appearance in Albany, New York. Dana had them drive to Canada from New York so they could make a few stops along the way to drop off money at the various businesses she ran. Their biggest drop was in Albany. She had three check cash centers there and they all did a lot of business.

They had just unloaded four hundred thousand dollars in cash. Their next stop was the mall. Annie hated working with Cory. He was always trying to make advances toward her. He may have had a chance if his breath didn't stink and if she hadn't found out who he really was. Still, she had no choice but to work with him. They finally pulled into the mall parking lot. Annie pushed her phone into her bag and got out of the SUV.

Annie had dyed her hair strawberry blond. Her hair was parted in the center of and pulled back into a ponytail that rested on her left shoulder, and flirted with her bosom as she walked. She wore a white sun visor with the letters BK in pink. Her white nylon body skirt had pink candy stripes and stopped midway down her thigh; it seemed to be making love to her frame as she moved. Along with that, she sported white on white Delta Force Nikes with no socks. Her well-toned calves and thighs looked moist from her body lotion. Her butt looked like a pillow stuffed with goose feathers, soft and fluffy. Annie was so busy looking in the different stores that she never noticed all the attention she was receiving.

Annie glided alongside Cory feeling as if she didn't have a care in the world. Suddenly, she felt someone grab her wrist. Her first thought was that someone was trying to snatch the Anne Klein watch with the diamond bezel and pink band she wore. She quickly pulled her wrist away and turned to face the assailant. She found herself face-to-face with the hip hop version of Brad Pitt. The Caucasian kid wore a tilted Red Sox fitted, a white tank top, over-sized grey sweatpants, and red and blue retro Jordan's. He had a thick gold link around his neck with a charm shaped like a toilet bowl with a diamond seat.

"Cupid dun shot me. I come to you seeking medical attention. Can you help me?" he said.

Annie was speechless. She didn't know what to say. A white boy had never tried to get at her before. He was bold enough to grab her wrist and his pickup line was delivered smoothly and confidently. Annie was both shocked and flattered. She looked to Cory for assistance. Cory cocked her head to one side, shrugged his shoulders, and folded his arms across his chest. He was at ease but he could have the Glock that was hidden on his waistline out in no time if something went wrong. Annie decided to flirt with the white boy.

"What's good, buttacup? You got every dude in here scared of you. Look at me I'm shaking like a leaf…," he said extending his hand and working his wrist back and forth.

"I'm scared but I ain't no coward. I know who you are. Does a white boy have a chance with a rap star?"

Annie studied him. *He was cute but, damn! He was white!*

"Have you ever been with a black girl before?" Annie blurted out before she knew what she was saying.

The white boy took his right index finger, made an X across the left side of his chest, and then held his right palm up.

"I'm a virgin. You'd be my first," he said with a smile.

Annie smiled, too, as did Cory.

"I didn't mean to ask you that. It just kind of slipped out," she said and offered her hand. "My name is Annie."

The white boy took her hand and replied, "Like I said, I know who you are. My name's Mark. I love what God's done with you. You could be your own religion. I'd turn my life over to you. I'm not gonna play myself and ask for your number. I mean, how does one call heaven? But will you accept my number?"

Annie smiled.

"What this be 'bout?" she asked.

She touched the charm on his chain checking the weight. The piece was solid.

"This," Mark said fingering the piece, "is my life story.

I've been pissed on and dumped on my whole life. I wear this to remind me that shit happens to everybody."

Cory was growing restless next to Annie.

"Look you gonna take the kid's number or what?" he asked sucking his teeth.

Mark handed Annie a small business card.

"What you do for a living?" she asked after studying the card.

"I design programs for computer software companies from the comfort of my home."

"Okay, Mark, I'm sure she'll call you. We gotta go," Cory said grabbing Annie's arm.

Annie looked over her shoulder as Cory led her away. Mark was rooted to the spot with his hands clasped together in a hopeful gesture. Annie smiled.

*****

The cameraman focused in on the diamond sitting in between Camecca's breasts and then started his pull back shot as she moved her body to the music echoing in the warehouse. Fahkirah was dancing alongside her looking into another camera as she sang along with the lyrics to Straight Slit, their latest single.

Tina wanted to take a different direction with them creatively this time with their videos. She knew the visual marketing was key in effecting album sales and building a new fan base. Their first album they released hadn't hidden their sexual preference. It had all the rainbows and lambda symbols.

This time around she wanted them to expose more of their sexuality rather than their preference. They had gained a huge fan base but in order to keep and expand it they needed to reach a little further. They had to sell optimism with individuality.

Tina had started handling a lot more artists and responsibility for A.B.J. They liked way she handled business for her clients and they loved her direction on music overall. They couldn't hire her because it would be a conflict of interest for her artist but after she had incorporated her management company into an entertainment group they were able to hire her on commission for certain projects.

She could tell Camecca was uncomfortable in the skin-tight leather cat suit with the wide butterfly collar. The zipper that ran from the waist was open almost halfway down exposing the mounds of her 38 C's. Her camel toe was desert ready! Tina had told her how hot she looked before she walked onto set.

Fahkira was a different story. She looked very comfortable and seemed all too willing to let it all hang out. She had shown up at the video shoot in a tennis mini that barely covered her buttocks. She worked the six inch heels as she pranced in front of the camera, bending and teasing. She fondled her breast through the cotton material of the white blouse she wore. The fact she hadn't worn a bra was obvious as the videographer captured her image.

Tina watched the duo. She would have never been able to market or promote a video like this back when she had first discovered her love for hip-hop. She felt a little guilty, at times, about her involvement with certain clients and their representation of the art. The truth was she was just a small screw on a big machine. She had to keep turning out hits and sex sells.

Tina had started getting hands on with the projects. She was thinking of going after an executive position at A.B.J. She hired a few people she had met over the last year or so that she could trust to handle things for her at her office while she oversaw the direction of certain projects and forged a relationship with the label. She already had a reputation as a good business woman.

She had once feared that the things the Hustle Kingz did would hurt her. It didn't. She had grown into her own woman in this industry. Love blinded you to so many things, even how strong your own legs were. *Once you realize you're standing up. You can walk away.*

When Trey and she had both started living their dreams, she never imagined she would wake up to this. She dreamed of doing what she was doing now all her life. She never thought it would be on such a grand scale, but she had dreamed this big. Now she wanted to accomplish her other dreams; and she just couldn't do that with Trey.

She was glad that her work kept her away from home a lot because home wasn't home anymore anyway. Trey was out on the road as much as she was or slipping away with Dana. She had known and had come to accept it for what it was. She just hadn't let go yet.

Her mother had always told her that when she fell in love she'd know it because she'd feel the coldness of the concrete nipping at her heart. Tina was caught in a bitter blizzard, battling against her own feelings and struggling to admit the other woman had won. Her mother had all the lessons on how to stay away from love but none on how to keep it.

Her mother had never kept any man around long enough for her to remember his name. She had taken her and her sister down to Harlem on a few occasions and pointed out their dad. Sometimes he was alone, other times he would be with his other family. There was a little girl and boy. They favored Michell and her.

On those expeditions her mother would really tell them how evil and deceptive men could be and how a woman could know and be willing to accept. Love was like an alcoholic beverage. You had to know your limits. It's important to recognize when you've had too much before you even sit at the bar.

She hadn't known her mother spoke from experience until she had become living proof. All the doubts Tina had before disappeared the morning she had told Trey that his grandfather had died. She picked him up from the airport later that day.

Trey had arrived on a flight from L.A. His face was full of grief but his scent revealed his guilt. When they embraced, Tina had smelled a hint of the body lotion she knew Dana wore. She hadn't said a word. She simply picked up the shattered pieces of her heart and had been holding them ever since hoping he'd help her piece it back together. He never did.

Deep down she knew he had been gone. Even if he stayed, he would be forever gone because the things she had seen for them were so far away now. She had played all her excuses and still produced a losing hand but she had learned a valuable lesson. Tina learned the one lesson her mother had never taught he, because she had never learned it herself: she deserved better.

Tina was ready to settle down now. She was ready to build a relationship with a man who loved her. She was ready to build a home that required no keys where he always felt welcomed and always wanted to be there. She was ready to build a family.

"Cut. That was great, girls. Why don't we call it a day? Great job, everyone!" Skip, the video director screamed.

Steve Lyons stepped up next to Tina clapping his

hands. "Hey, beautiful. You still think you're in love with a rapper?"

"I'm almost certain."

Steve Lyons was "6 4' with a dark caramel complexion. He had hazel eyes and a clean-shaven head that was shaped perfectly. He kept his goatee neatly trimmed and his nails manicured. This was the man her grandmother had told her to bring home. He was one of the chief executives over at A.B.J., one of the few brothers with a top position. He had a house in the Hamptons, was intelligent, and earned seven figures a year.

Tina had made her first million on her own though. She'd snatched an opportunity while she was in school and had made a career salary in less than two years. She wasn't disappointed with what she had become. Tina was a caterpillar. She was ready to break out of her cocoon and see what she had really become.

Neither one of them moved as people went about breaking down the set. She smiled. Steve had been after her for the last seven months. He was close enough for Tina to smell his cologne. He always smelled good and was handsome like nobody's tomorrow.

"Nice shoes. What are you? About a seven in little boys?" he asked pointing down at her Prada pumps.

"What you say?"

Tina thought about the old man in the shoe store. What was it he had said? *'The man that knows your shoe size at a glance. Will turn you into Cinderella.'*

"I'm about a seven or eight-"

"Depending on how the shoe fits," he said finishing her sentence.

"Yeah, right."

"After watching this all day, you gotta be hungry. Let

me buy you supper."

She thought about where Trey was, or rather, where he was supposed to be, Denver, Colorado. The Hustle Kingz were doing a show out there and then headed to Vegas. Who would see her and report her movements? It could be business. She was nervous taking too long to answer. Steve was staring at her.

"I can eat."

"Good. I know a nice spot not too far from here in Chelsea. The food's great and there's karaoke. Did you drive?"

"No, I rode with Camecca. Let me go in the back and let the girls' know I'm leaving."

"Okay, cool."

He watched her walk back to the dressing area on the set. He couldn't help but smile and shake his head before heading out the door.

Tina walked into the dressing room and Fahkira looked up from the bag she was sifting through.

"We on our way out. I'm just looking for my phone."

"It's cool. I'm gonna catch a ride with Steve."

"Um. That's why you bust through the door looking like the Kool-Aid man." Camecca said.

"Girl, knock it off." Tina grinned harder.

"You was cheesin' though. Here go my shit," Fahkira said pulling her phone out of the bag.

"Y'all crazy. I'll see y'all later. Call me."

"Ain't nobody crazy. We know how crazy that fool ass nigga got you. We your girls. You deserve better for real though," Camecca said.

"Yes, you do," Fahkira chimed in.

"Thanks, ladies. I'll see y'all later."

"Later," they said in unison.

They rode to the restaurant in Steve's 740I BMW. He put the radio on the jazz station and didn't say too much. The restaurant was nice. Tina had never even noticed it before which surprised her since she was often in Chelsea.

When they were seated, Steve ordered a bottle of red wine. This is how she always pictured her dates. The linen table cloths and fine China no longer impressed her. She had antique cabinets full of it. She sought this atmosphere and being with the right person.

"So, when you gonna come over to the winning team?" Steve asked with a smile.

"Am I losing?"

"Not really but you messing with a loser. Dude is not your type."

"How would you know that? You know my type?"

"I know that you are too much of a woman to walk around and let a boy who hasn't grown up yet treat you like less than a woman. The whole industry is whispering about it."

"Everyone's whispering because they're speculating."

"There not though. It's a shitty deal but that's how things work in the industry. We'll show clean teeth and whisper about your dirt after you've left the room."

"Is that what you're doing now?"

"No, Tina. I'm trying to take you home to my mother and then take you to our home and make babies with you."

"Make babies. Our home?"

"I'm serious. I've watched you for a long time. Let me make you happy. You don't need an entertainer. You need a man."

"Are you that man?" Tina said with a raised a brow.

"Hell yeah. Let me break this down for you. I'm thirty-five. You're twenty-six."

She looked surprised.

"Yeah, boo, I did my homework."

"Boo," She batted her eyes and smiled.

"Yeah, boo! Look. I'm serious. I know dude might be your childhood sweetheart but he's still a child. Where he's at, I've been there. I played my games already. Had the groupies, blown millions on things that weren't as exciting as when the other guys Bugatti zoomed up the runway. I've taken all my flights. I'm ready to land. I'm more settled. I need a wife. You competing with a cup and a crazy broad right now. You can always be winning, but why fight if you don't have to?"

"A wife!"

Tina's outburst caused some patrons from another table to look over at their table. The woman butchering Melanie Fiona's *It Kills Me* hadn't seemed to notice.

"Yeah, it's that serious right now. I'm that serious."

"You don't even know me."

"But I do. You just won't take the time to get to know me."

The waiter returned with their wine and filled their glasses.

How about this? We both agree to give it some time to get to each other better

Steve held up his glass for a toast. Tina clinked crystal with him and sipped.

"We can do that."

Chapter 14

Pain, Fame & Work

Trey was being interviewed in front of the Hustle Kingz' tour bus outside the Staple Center. He was amped up because they he was going to be performing on stage tonight with the Hustle Kingz in front of a crowd of almost twenty thousand. Maze pinched the brim of his fitted, pulled it up and down on his forehead, looked into the camera, and started clapping his hands together as he spoke.

"Yo, check it out! It's ya boy Trey and I'm here with Salasi from Eye On The Street DVD, Harlem's own out here in Cali with the swag that's oh so real. Shout to the whole West Coast. You know how we doin' it, Hustle Kingz World Domination! It's the take-over. Shout to Land Pirates. They just did they thing on stage."

"How has it been touring with them?"

"It's all love. We go from state to state fuckin' groupies, getting' money, and smokin' that good green. And, of course, I'm drinkin' good."

Trey held up his cup and waved a bag of weed in front of the camera.

"Shout to Cali again. We love you," he said as he ran the bag of high grade marijuana across his upper lip.

"There's been a lot of talk from Anonymous and his peoples in response to you guys saying they snitched on your man. What's up with that?"

"I mean people know what it is. That's a true song. You feel me? We in the streets, so we know what it is. You don't hear no incidents with us havin' issues"

Trey stretched his arms out at his sides.

"Look. We out in Cali right now. I ain't got no security. The jewels is right. Ain't nothin'. Feel me?"

He grabbed at the four chains on his neck and shook the jewelry. Took a pull on his Tarantula and blew smoke into the screen.

"I mean come on, man. We live the best life. We everywhere and we can show our face. Since his man snatched that little chain and his other man told they gotta be easy breeze in the town. Ya dig?"

"So, are you sayin' they can't perform?"

"Naw, I'm not sayin' that. They just had a show in Arizona two nights ago but that's the label being strategic settin' up shows for them. Movin' them around us quietly. Spot checkin' for dough according to our tour schedule. We ain't bumpin' into them dudes nowhere, and they don't be out nowhere. Check photogram. You see people posting pics wit' me and my cup everywhere."

"So, you think if your clique crossed path with them there would be an issue?"

"What clique? I am by myself. Look at me! I'm not worried 'bout dude. I'm getting' paper. When I leave her tonight I'm goin' to sleep on Charlotte Thomas sheets with gold threadin' with some five star pussy."

"I feel you son. The peoples is feeling you. We feeling

you. Give the people one last shout out and let them know who you with."

"Yo, like I said. I'm here with my man Salasi from Eye On The Streets DVD make sure you get your copies at all the local retailers, ya moms and pop shops, and all over the hood! It's ya boy, the world's finest, Trey-Eight. Spin the barrel. Bang you're a star,"

Trey made a gun out of his hand and winked.

Salasi turned off the camera and gave him dap.

"Yo, good lookin', my dude. I'm gonna get this to editing tomorrow and we should have it out the first of next month."

"No doubt. Just keep me posted."

"I got you."

Trey walked on the tour bus and took a sip from his cup. He looked around at everybody on the bus. Maze and Boogs were joking around with some groupies. Fogg was in the back playing around in the studio. Dudes he knew and some he didn't know where all over the place.

Trey made his way through the chaos to his private room and went inside. He sat on the bed and took another sip from his cup. He thought about the road he had traveled to become what others' called successful. He was tired of playing the role and getting in front of the camera. He just wanted to rap. It was ironic how it took so much to do something that came to him with ease.

There were millions of kids that wanted to live his life and he didn't even want it anymore. Dana was pressuring him from all angles. She wanted another multi-platinum album from him and the Hustle Kingz. She threatened to expose her pregnancy to Tina and she was trying to force him to sign over his publishing for the next album.

Trey decided to tell Tina about the affair. He knew she

would be crushed when she learned Dana was pregnant but they would work through it somehow. She loved him. They had been distant lately, but he doubted seriously she had strayed. They had been through so much together.

Trey had kept Dana quiet so far by getting out on the road and doing shows. He had cut her in on his end for twenty percent. Tina had told him how grimy Dana was, but he hadn't listened. She had cut off their sex and, frankly, he didn't miss it. He remembered how cold he had felt lying next to her after Tina had called and told him they had found his grandfather dead in his apartment of an overdose. She had barely expressed concern before rolling over to go to sleep.

Trey had left the next morning with the papers that had sealed his fate. He had even stopped threatening paternity tests. He knew she hadn't been sleeping around. They were always together. He hadn't told Boogs of his dilemma. He had been too busy hanging out with Maze and chasing groupies to notice. Fogg was in love with somebody he refused to bring around and, knowing this industry, Trey couldn't blame him. Bigga was managing a lot of different up and coming talent now. So, he wasn't around as much. It was like everyone he had started with was no longer around even though they were standing in the same room. It really did seem like it was just him and his cup sometimes. Trey tilted the cup and drained the contents.

"Yo where Cory disappear to. He found him a personal groupie?" Trey asked one of their roadies, Torrance.

"Naw. I think he said he had to make some runs for Dana."

"She will keep niggas running around for her as long as they got legs."

Torrance smiled. "I'd like to run up in her. Then maybe

I can get off the road. It's too much sometimes."

"I know what you mean." Trey said as he refilled his cup.

*****

"What you got over there?"

"One point five," Dana said.

"A'ight perfect. I got one point seven over here," Bigga said.

Dana started putting the money in the duffel bag. She and Bigga and Annie had been counting money for the last nine hours. He had come to her with the scheme of washing his illicit funds eight months ago.

Dana had the connections and the intelligence to set up an elaborate and lucrative money laundering business. His dope profits went through the spin cycle twice, but it was worth it. It was better to pay someone to clean the dirty cash than to have the Feds sitting around monitoring your spending.

Annie was working her magic as always. Bigga had been flirting with her the entire time. Her jeans fit like a fresh coat of body paint and her charming smile to all his jokes had made him lose count more than once. Dana hadn't missed a note. She had beat him to the tune of a hundred grand while he was spitting game.

Dana looked up and saw Bigga patting his hand against Annie's ass as she put money in a duffel bag. She smiled. They all fell for Annie. She had been instrumental in a lot of the moves Dana had made in the industry. Annie was another one of her stars. She had taken her in when she was thirteen.

Scheme had brought her to the studio one day and she wandered from the lounge into the recording session. Dana saw her and was immediately struck by her beauty. She had thought she was his young cousin or something. That was not the case.

Annie was a runaway from Spartanburg, South Carolina. She'd been attracted to the bright lights of the city like a moth, but not at all prepared for the flame. She had been stashed away in a Brownsville apartment as entertainment for Scheme and his homies in the hood. She had been surviving on corner store hero sandwiches and fifty cent pops.

Dana saw her potential immediately. Not for rap; she was a terrible rapper. Annie was smart. She was an excellent student. She could be instructed. Dana had taken her under her wing. She got her away from the goons she had been hanging around and put her in a place where her potential could really pay off.

Dana had changed her life and Annie, in turn, changed hers. She was forever faithful, and never complained. Most people thought she was just fine flesh and giggles, to Dana she was much more.

"Yo, is this shit real, shortie?"

"You feel it. You know it's real." Annie turned and stuck her tongue out at Bigga.

"Shit, I know chicks that got doctors that have shit feeling so official."

She sucked her teeth.

"Auntie, will you tell this boy this ass is all mine."

"Oh, yeah. That's God's work right there. Same bottom I use to change when she was a kid."

"Umm. I want to change her," Bigga said.

"Boy, you ain't ready. You just a kid that want candy 'cause he see it."

He clapped his hands together, shook his head, and

licked his lips.

"I promise you. Won't be no kidding around with me. I got that tap out dick."

"You and every other nigga."

Dana listened to them go back and forth as she started sending out the texts to her peoples out west to get the washing machine started. Dana had perfected the art of making money disappear then reappear somewhere else. Her system was foolproof.

There were three basic steps to laundering cash. The first step was getting the money entered into a financial market that is legitimate. This step is called placing. The next step in the process, probably the most difficult, is to move the money around to remove any traces of its true source. Let the cash flow, so to speak. This is called layering. The final step is *integrating*. Once the funds have mingled with legitimate funds long enough, they could be integrated into the true flow of things. It was like a gang initiation and Dana was the fearless leader.

Dealing with the label for so many years had taught her how to be really criminal. It had taught her how to steal like the ones that never got their collars dirty. Handling budgets for tens of millions of dollars had showed her the system. She had learned how money moved and how it worked. Most artists had no clue what they were supposed to get, even when it was written on paper right in front of them.

Talent was a funny thing. It had to have the right placement in order to be worth anything. Some people spend their entire lives working at something they're good at but neglect their true talent. Dana knew she wasn't a singer or rapper. She was talented at manipulation and seduction. She was a Brooklyn girl.

She refused to be a victim or a vehicle for another man's success without making sure her place was set at the table as well. The men in this industry were treacherous. She had witnessed so many so called video vixens abused by entertainers waiting to get their moment to shine, only to end up in the dark getting groped and sexually abused by wolves. She had seen it all but she had been a victim of none of it.

The 2.9 Bigga was giving her would get her quick four hundred thousand. She had networks set up all over the states. It was her own network that she had built. She had started by opening small grocery stores, check cash centers, and car washes, any business that dealt a with lot of cash and appeared legitimate. After the front companies were in place she started running the illicit funds through them. Cash on hand was harder to trace than a swipe of the credit card.

There were multiple ways for her to mix the money up, such as playing the stock market or buying property under market value with cash and reselling at full value. The cash became the other guy's problem and most of them wanted to duck Uncle Sam's haymaker. So they would just stash the loot away. Dana never skipped out on Uncle Sam's capital gains tax. You can never expect to take it all. The world was too big and who would you share it with. Dana put the last of the bills in the duffel bag and zipped it up.

"Did our other package make it to Cali safely?" Bigga asked.

He had given Dana $1.5 million a month ago for her to send out West to the front companies she had set up for him. He had been trying to figure out how she was moving the money around, but he hadn't cracked that.

When he did he could stop paying her a handler's fee. He hated the thought of being handled.

"Yup. It sure did. I spoke with the promoter's in Cali earlier. Everything is straight."

Dana was using the same method the artists who had been caught with the dope dealer used to transfer the bills. Hydraulic lifts beneath the tour buses. She had people set up in all the locations she needed to retrieve the money. She figured the Feds would never get wise to her movements. After all, she wasn't moving narcotics.

They exited the studio and went to their separate cars. Annie followed Bigga. Dana honked her horn at the security guard in the booth as he saluted her.

As soon as she had made her turn and Bigga made his in the opposite direction, Gregory came out of the booth and went into the building where the studios were housed. He checked the footage on the hidden surveillance system he had installed. After watching the first twenty minutes of the video, he stopped it and called Lanno.

"What you got for me, Gregory?" Lanno said when he answered the line.

"I got our nigger red handed stealing."

"Are you sure?"

"I just got done watching her and the other creep that's been working with the label counting a studio full of cash. There was at least two million dollars."

There was a long pause and then a sigh.

"You know what to do. Don't leave any loose ends.

"I won't. What are you going to do about getting someone to run the label?"

"That's my business. You just handle yours."

"Yes, sir."

Gregory ended the call. He was going to have to time

his moves perfectly. Dana always kept someone around her. Still, there was always a way and he always found it.

Chapter 15

It's the Ones that Smoke Blunts wit' Cha...

Fogg felt good as he rolled up to his projects in the chauffeured Bentley. He stepped with his platinum chain flooded with diamonds. The whole neighborhood was out. Today was the day everyone celebrated a young neighborhood gangster, White Boy, who had been killed back in the day. He had called ahead and had spoken to Terell. He had the hood on lock. He controlled all the major distribution of narcotics in the neighborhood or he collected rent from the other drug crews in and around the neighborhood.

Terell was standing with Keith Douglas and a few other guys he didn't recognize as the chauffer opened his door. He stepped out with a smile pasted on his lips and his latest mix-tape *Boogie Down Killers*, in his hand. It had been released under A.B.J. through a deal Tina had set up. The disc was already platinum. The smell of barbeque and the sound of music came from the other side of the basketball courts where a tournament game was going on. It felt good to be back home.

He had finally become something. It wasn't a deal with

a label like he had first dreamed of but he was happy he had listened to Tina. He was more famous and making more money working freelance. He was one of the most sought after producers in the industry. It felt good to be able to return to the hood as a success story.

He hoped by the time he was thirty he could be out the industry and living somewhere in a small town in Maine. He loved his neighborhood but growing up here had made him want to get away. There was always seemed to be so much sorrow and despair. In a city of millions, Fogg was one of the many souls that felt alone.

Fogg extended his hand and gave Terell dap. "What's good?"

"You, big time producer," Terell Bag said with a smirk and looking at Keith.

"I know, right. You rollin' up to the projects in a Bentley and shit. You wanna show muthafuckas you made it, huhn?" Keith said.

"Man, I'm just tryin' to live," Fogg said.

Terell looked at the other two guys standing around them before reaching for the disc Fogg held.

"This the joint?"

"Yeah," Fogg said cheesing.

Terell opened the cover and read the shout outs and thank yous. *To my long-time friend and a true boss of bosses, Terell. Fogg.* He smiled and handed the disc to Keith.

"Yo, you got that herb son?" he said to one of the guys standing with them.

"Yeah," the tall, burly, dark skinned guy said.

"Yo, let's go in the buildin' real quick and smoke this herb real quick. I wanna holla at you 'bout some shit anyway," Terell said looking at the chauffer who was still standing on the sidewalk near the Bentley.

"A'ight," Fogg said. He waved to the chauffer and said to him, "I'll be right back. Just chill in the car."

The chauffer nodded and they walked off toward the building.

"Yo, this my homies, Peeto and Slim," Terell Bag said introducing the two guys.

"A'ight. What's up?" Fogg said giving each man dap.

"Hey, man, so you be fuckin' dem stars and shit. Who you dun hit man?" Peeto asked.

Fogg smiled and thought about Annie. She had been distant toward him lately but that was his boo. He really could see himself settling down with her after all the lights went out.

"A few but I never kiss and tell. You feel me?"

"Nigga, you might as well tell somebody. You wasn't spankin' dimes before you got dem coins," Terell laughed and reached for a dap from Keith.

"Hells yeah. 'Member that time we paid that crack head to suck all the l'il niggas off on the roof. This l'il nigga was shook," Keith laughed.

"Man, fuck y'all niggas. I wasn't trying to let that nasty bitch touch me. Now, it's nothing but platinum coated wombs. Ya dig!"

"Naw, we still fuckin' these good ole project bitches," Trey laughed.

"Man, this nigga was a nerd," Keith said laughing as the elevator opened on the seventh floor.

"Yeah, right. I just went to school."

"Like I said, nigga," Keith said continuing to laugh.

They walked to an apartment at the end of the hall. Fogg could smell the remnants of Kush in the air soon as he stepped into the apartment. They headed into the living room and Slim ran right for the X Box controller. Terell shook his head and walked to the back of the apartment.

Peeto lit the herb and sat next to Fogg on the loveseat. The smell of the marijuana exploded in the area immediately. Peeto took two deep pulls on the blunt and passed it to Fogg. Soon as he hit the herb his chest exploded and his lungs got hot. He started choking, and went to pass the herb without hitting it again.

Just as he was passing the blunt Terell came around the corner holding an AR-15. Before Fogg could say anything he felt the barrel of a gun being stuffed in his side. He froze.

"You know what it is nigga. Where the money?" Terell said.

Fogg's mind was racing. All he had on him was two hundred and ten dollars. He didn't carry cash on him like that. What were there fools thinking? He wasn't the dope boy from up the block with stacks on deck. He did his business with banks, not the disenfranchised. Why had he come back around here?

"Hey, man, stop... stop playing, man," Fogg stammered.

He felt a hard blow to his head.

"You think this shit a game, nerd ass nigga!" Peeto said.

"Yeah, mister super producer. You thought you was gonna come back 'round here all caked up and hand niggas a disc?" "I ain't gonna ask you again to come up off that paper," Keith said.

"Give me my weed, nigga." Peeto said grabbing the blunt and pressing the pistol back into Fogg's side.

Fogg dug in his pockets and pulled out the two hundred and ten dollars.

"All the money, nigga, and hurry up," Terell said gripping the assault rifle tighter.

"I don't got no more money. I swear to God," he cried.

"Muthafucka, you come round here in a Bentley, dressed all fly and shit, and you sayin' you ain't got no money? Muthafucka, we seen you on TV. We seen the money, nigga."

"That shit be for show man. It ain't like that. I swear!" Fogg said lying.

"Well, nigga, you 'bout to die for frontin'" Terell said and put a menacing look on his face as he had started squeezing the trigger.

"Wait, man, please wait…"

* * * * *

Trey was walking out the juice spot when his phone rang. It was Tina. He thought about the ten ounces of syrup he had in the bag and started to ignore the call but changed his mind.

"What's up?"

"Trey."

She sounded like she was crying. He was preparing himself to hear another one of her rants about him screwing Dana behind her back and making her look like a fool in the industry.

"Yeah, who else gonna be answering my phone?"

"They…"

She paused for a long moment.

"They who? What the fuck is up?" he barked.

"They killed Fogg."

Trey stopped walking.

"What? Who killed Fogg?"

"Nobody knows. It happened in his projects. It's on the news now."

Trey hurried toward his Benz.

"What the fuck was he doing in the projects?"

"They had that tournament game up there today for White Boy."

"Fuck. I'm on my way up there. I'm gonna hit you back."

He hung up without waiting for her to respond. He jumped in the Benz tossing the bag of syrup in the passenger seat. He called Boogs and got a busy signal. He tried again, before throwing the phone in the passenger seat and starting the Benz. He pulled out the parking space and made a wild U-turn heading uptown.

Miller and Holmes had been sitting in a black on black Suburban across from the syrup house. They had been trailing Trey all day and, so far, the day had been uneventful. It looked like the phone call he just took got his gears going.

"What do you think it is?" Holmes asked as he started the SUV and pulled into traffic trailing the Benz.

"Who the hell knows? Whatever it is he's trying to get there. I say we pull 'em and ruin his day. We know he has narcotics in the car he just came from Mrs. Butterworth's main plant. Light the grill up at the next light."

Holmes pressed on the gas and caught up with the Benz. He waited until the light caught them on 145th street and turned on the lights in the SUV's grill. Both of the detectives jumped out with their guns drawn and moved toward Trey's vehicle.

Miller saw him trying to reach for the bag of syrup. He tapped the passenger glass with the barrel of his gun and smiled before breaking the glass with his pistol and aiming the gun at Trey.

"Stop moving, muthafucka, or I'll make you a fallen

star," Miller said.

Holmes pulled open the driver's side door, pulled Trey out, and threw him to the ground. Pedestrians stopped to see what was going on when they recognized Trey.

"What the fuck is this?" Trey demanded.

Holmes pressed a knee in his back while he applied his handcuffs extra tightly and replied, "This is an arrest young man. You are in possession of narcotics."

"C'mon, man. My homie just got killed in The Bronx, man. Write me a ticket and go catch some real criminals."

"You look like you have a few ounces of the syrup here, Trey. You can't get a ticket for this. You can get three to five," Miller said, holding up the bag.

"I tell you what. We'll let you go right now if you tell us how Dana is moving the dope around from state to state."

"Man, I don't know what the fuck you're talking about no drugs. Fuck you."

"You want us to call somebody to get your car from the impound? 'Cause you're not getting any special treatment this time. Since we know you're not going to talk to us, we're taking you straight to booking. You're going through the system."

"Man, fuck y'all!" Trey screamed.

"Getting geared up for the men you gonna be sleeping with, huhn?" Miller asked as Holmes lead him back to the SUV.

Trey called Tina as soon as he got to the precinct. He told her to go get the car out of impound before he was hauled off to a cell full of other inmates. The detectives had tried to scare him when they had put him in the cell by telling him he was going to be raped before morning. They couldn't have been more wrong. The guys in the cell showed him love. They stayed up all night asking questions and singing their favorite song lyrics he'd written. He kept the inmates entertained, but he spent the entire time wondering who had killed Fogg.

By the time an officer came to tell him he was being released, he had lost track of time. It felt like he had been in the cell for days, but actually it had been only twelve hours. When Trey stepped out the holding area, he saw Tina.

She had been crying. He figured she'd take Fogg's death hard. They had been close. Dana was walking up behind Tina along with the label's lawyer. He opened his arms as Tina walked up to him. Tina stopped and stared at Trey's outstretched arms. Her eyes were dark, her body rigid.

"What's wrong with you?"

Tina pulled some papers from her bag and threw them into Trey's face just as Dana stepped up to them.

"What's wrong with me? You got this bitch pregnant?" Tina screamed pointing in Dana's direction.

"Look, missy, I don't-"

Dana never got to finish her sentence. Tina grabbed a fist full of her hair and jerked her head downward into a right uppercut. Dana reached out trying to grab her as she hit her with another uppercut. Dana fell to the floor as Tina started kicking her in her side and stomach screaming Bitch repeatedly.

It took Trey and the attorney a moment to respond. By the time they started trying to grab Tina, police officers were running from every direction. After Tina had been restrained by the police and Dana was helped to her feet, she looked at Tina and said, "You're dead, bitch. You killed my baby!"

"Fuck you and your dead baby, bitch. You can have that nigga, too. I'm done! Done! You hear me, muthafucka!"

Tina continued to scream as the police dragged her away. A few of the officers tried to comfort, Dana. They helped her to a seat until EMS could arrive. Trey looked at Dana and the attorney before walking away.

Fogg was buried five days later. It seemed like the entire industry came out to his funeral. Everyone was there, except Tina. She had been arrested for assaulting Dana and there was a restraining order in place that prevented her from coming within a thousand feet of Dana. Dana had been certain to make it known to the police that were working the funeral detail that if they saw Tina she was to be arrested on sight.

After the repast, Boogs Cory, and Trey headed to Harlem to meet with Maze and Bigga. They met in one of Bigga's old spots on 132nd Street. They had gotten a line on who had robbed and killed Fogg. Apparently one of the guys involved was wearing the chain they had taken from him around the neighborhood.

"Yo, I heard Terell and Keith Douglas were the ones that were involved. I know them dudes from outs Moorehouses," Boogs said.

"Yeah, I know them cats, too. Terell just got picked up the other day by the Feds. He had a little crew going out to Alabama," Bigga said.

"Man, fuck dat. What we gonna do? We can't have niggas running 'round talkin' 'bout they robbed us. We need to hit dat other nigga before the Feds get him, too. This will be the second time niggas dun took some shit from niggas." Maze said.

"Whoa! That other shit is gettin' handled, dude!" Boogs said shooting Maze a look.

"When, nigga? Man, you talkin' dat shit for months. I ain't seen no results yet. Dat bitch probably got you marked, nigga!"

Boogs started advancing toward Maze. Bigga stepped between the two men.

Trey stepped out of the shadows of the room. He took a sip from his cup.

"What's that gonna do? Y'all two niggas fighting. Getting at these clowns. We," he looked at Boogs and continued, "I didn't sign up for this. We gangsta rappers, not gangsters. My nigga is gone and so is my lady."

He took another sip from his cup. He stuffed his right hand in his suit pocket and walked out the apartment leaving the four of them standing there.

Trey walked outside and stood on the sidewalk. He looked around. Kids were running between cars playing chase. The old men had a table set up under a lamppost playing dominos. Women sat on stoops discussing the petty things in life. In between gossip they lifted an eye to watch the children. The hustlers perched near the corner keeping an eye out for police.

Trey breathed in a deep breath and then exhaled. This was the life he knew. When he had been here everything had been alright. He was amongst the many other dreamers. Once he had moved amongst the stars, his world had turned dark.

He didn't want to believe it though. He took out a Newport and lit it. Blowing the smoke toward stars that lit up the night sky. He pulled out his phone and called Michell. She answered on the third ring.

"What's up?"

He could tell by her voice she wasn't feeling him. But at least she had taken his call.

"Yo, Tina trippin'. She won't-."

"What, my nigga." Michell said cutting him off, "You

trippin', my nigga. My sister was the best thing that ever happened to you. Wasn't nobody judging you as you claim. Yeah, she told me all the shit you said about my grandmother and all the other shit you been carrying around in your heart. Once my sister started shining."

"It wasn't like that."

"Oh, really? How was it then? You got your boss pregnant, right?"

There was a long pause and then the sound of Michell exhaling and sucking her teeth came through the line.

"Like I said, my nigga. I'm on the phone with you. My sister don't want to talk to you all fine and dandy. But I'm gonna give you the benefit of the doubt. I'm gonna hear your side. So far, you ain't said shit worth listening to. That's why I keep talking. So what happened? You an expectant father or not?"

"Yo, Chell. You right. I fucked up. I took your sister for granted. It's this industry. This fuckin' syrup. That shit be having me in mood swings and shit. You know I love your sister."

"I'm sure she has love for you, too, because that's just the type of person she is. But I'm gonna just keep it G with you, homie. She has moved on. You let this industry make a whore out of you. She refuses to let you make a fool out of her. Just let her go. Just move on and continue to strive for greatness. Caution your steps. You'll always be able to look back and say; I used to love her."

Michell ended the call without waiting for him to respond. The truth was he really didn't have a response. She was right. Tears stained his cheeks as he held the phone to his ear listening to silence.

Trey tilted his cup again and drank some of the syrupy liquid. He poured the rest into the street as he walked to his Benz. He got into the car took one more look around before he started the engine and pulled off.

Chapter 16

Trey had really been in a slump lately. He had been turning down shows and interviews left and right. The only time he left his home was when he had to. TMZ was talking about him leaving Tina and getting Dana pregnant. They made it seem like Dana and he were a couple but he hadn't even spoken to her directly since Fogg's funeral. He was starting to understand the flaws of fame and notoriety.

Annie said she knew someone who could get him charged back up. So, here he was sitting at his bar watching her home girl circle the pool table with the cue. Her name was Bunches. Annie had told him that she was mature for her age. He hadn't realized she meant mentally. She was a fine woman, but her mind was the center of attraction.

She had only been at the house twenty four hours and she had already started making him feel alive again. They hadn't even slept together the night before. They had stayed up talking about money, life, and love. She had been far more mature than he had given her credit for when he had picked her up at JFK. Her financial portfolio read like a Forbes article.

The thing that really got him is the story she had told

him how she had become a millionaire by age twenty. He didn't know whether the story was true or not but he knew it had all the elements of a hit record. Annie was right. He was ready to work again. He figured she had also known he would need her to play the female role, both in the studio and the video.

He smiled, picked up his rum and coke from the bar, and sipped. Bunches walked directly in his sights. Her back was turned as she looked at the balls on the purple felt. She bent over and stroked the cue as she measured up her shot. He could see her pussy was shaved when she lifted a leg from the ground to take the shot. Her pink gold flashed and caused a woody in his pants.

"Damn. I missed. I shoulda cut it a little more."

Bunches turned around looking dead in his eyes like she knew where they had just been focused. Her smile became more seductive as she blew a kiss in his direction.

"Your turn. I set you up for the eight ball, too."

"I think you just set me up," he said getting up and revealing the boner in his jeans.

"Well, damn! You got all types of sticks. I mean tricks," Bunches said laughing.

"Genetics," he laughed and picked up his cue.

Just as he was stepping away from the bar his phone vibrated. It was a text from Annie. He opened the text and began to read the message. He couldn't believe what he was reading.

He jumped up and screamed, "Yeah!"

"Well, damn. Which one of your groupies dun sent you a coochie shot?" Bunches asked smiling.

"Naw, it's not that. Yo, check this shit out. I love Annie, yo."

He passed the phone to Bunches and she looked at the

screen.

"Who's Dana Peterson?"

Trey looked at Bunches. He was surprised that she didn't know Annie's aunt, since she was Annie's girl.

"Some chick that was trying to get me in a paternity suit. But, it's all good now. I love Annie. That's my bitch!"

"That my bitch, too. But I ain't gonna front. She know I don't be fuckin' with no loose niggas. When I fall, I fall hard. My heart ain't nothing to play with. Now, if you just wanna kick it. You better grab the right stick before you take your shot."

She handed him back his phone. He looked at her in the short body skirt. He admired her young, gorgeous features. He thought about all the groupies he had been with in the states and abroad and then he thought about what Bunches said. He wasn't going to make the same mistake twice. He had loved and lost so he understood matters of the heart better.

"I'm gonna bank that eight ball in the side pocket. Soon as I thank Annie and send this message to my peoples at MTV. Yeah, baby!"

"You probably made the best choice. You betta not miss," Bunches said laughing.

"Naw, I'm feeling lucky," Trey said as he pressed send.

He brought the message back up on his screen and smiled as he read it again.

From: Annie O

To: Trey

Kings County Hospital

Dr. Derrick Bunzine.

After examining Miss Peterson post miscarriage. It has been determined eggs will no longer appear for fertilization so therefore all future attempts at procreation will be impossible; naturally or by any medical fertilization procedure.

Derrick Bunzine.

Trey went back to the bar and grabbed his cue. He leaned over the table and drew the cue back. The tip contacted the cue ball sending it smacking into the eight ball. The eight ball banged the side of the felt and head back toward the side pocket where Trey was standing.

"I told you I was feeling lucky."

* * * * *

The fax machine rattled. Holmes jumped up from his seat and grabbed the transcript that had just come through. Miller hadn't taken his eyes off the TV screen built into the back of the front passenger's seat of the Hummer. The screen was 28". It was something custom the department had thrown in to bling it out more in an effort to help their covert operations in the hip-hop community.

Miller shook his head and clapped his hands together and said, "Man, your boy, Trey, gotta be tapping this little bitch. Look at them in this video."

"Hey, our inside ear just got at us with some serious intel. I think these guys are planning to peel somebody's wig back!"

"Who?"

"Hey, Miller get your head back in the game. What are we doing here? Who the hell are you watching? The Hustle Kingz, man."

"Who they planning to take out?"

"Who the hell do you think man? Anonymous. It's

just like we said in the beginning. They can't let that chain incident that took place in Brooklyn go down like that."

"Yeah, this is the world of shooting stars," Miller chuckled.

He looked at the screen again where Annie was stepping through a strip club putting the best dancers to shame moving her body seductively.

"Damn, Annie. Looks like your boy going down for the old one two. I heard the rap ciphers on the yard. Has the energy of a Third World Country. Ain't that what that last slang speaking nigga we sent away said in the documentary? He shot from prison."

"Yeah, but all these guys are looking for the same thing, another chance to be on top. Most of them are dreamers. So, being hopeful that you can successfully come back and dominate the charts isn't reaching in their minds."

"Niggas ain't gonna get nowhere in this country until they at least learn how to pull their pants up and know that purple is a color and not a drink or a plant. These fucking idiots make millions destroying a language and we're stuck following them around."

"Well, at least we get to travel in style," Holmes said as he sent a fax back to the undercover agent they had working at Global.

"I'm a Cadillac man myself. We gonna play this one like we always do?"

"Yup, two birds with one stone."

"They'll find some more stars to put in the sky. The ghetto is full of silver linings but the stitching always seems off like a knock off bag."

"That's because the hood ain't an outlet mall. It's more like the corner store."

"Yeah and there's always those two guys in the back

making two dollar heroes."

"Yeah, but even a vegetarian must realize a plant has skin and the nutrients rest beneath."

"Damn, rappers got us talking in metaphors."

"Just stay on beat."

"I will," Miller said stealing another look at Annie on the screen.

"We're meeting our guy out in Brooklyn tonight. He has a little song bird for us to listen to."

"More like a mocking bird. All these gangster rappers are gangster right up to the point you push the mic in their face."

"Yeah, the same ole song."

Chapter 17

Once a Good Girl's Gone Bad, She's Gone Forever...

Tina stomped her feet lightly on the gold and burgundy carpet as she entered the lobby of the ski resort. Her dark grey, suede Timberland boots with the pink tree were size seven in boys. At first glance one may had even taken her for a child she was so short and bundled up. But the skin-tight grey suede denim pants she wore wouldn't be found in the kid's department of any store.

She removed the hood of her pink leather Bomber coat to reveal her silky smooth jet black hair. Her hair crowned her face giving an angelic glow to her features.

Steve stepped in behind her wearing a black leather coat with Elk fur around the collar. The hand-woven black turtleneck sweater he wore went well with his olive green corduroys and black Timberland boots.

He grabbed both sides of Tina's waist and began to usher her forward riding her rump as he did so. After they confirmed their reservation at the front desk, they were escorted with their luggage to their room.

Tina marveled at the size and décor of the room. The main room was done in earth tones. The furniture was neatly arranged around a glass table that held a black vase with fresh violets. In the far left corner was a fully stocked brass and marble bar equipped with all the tools for mixing drinks.

The center wall housed the room's entertainment center which included a 72" TV mounted to the wall, a DVD/CD player and state of the art surround sound. There was fireplace with neatly arranged logs on either side. Finally, right at the foot of the hearth, lay an authentic bear-skin rug.

Tina wandered off into the bedroom and was almost startled by the oversized bed. The top of the mattress had to be at least twelve by twelve. She felt herself shrinking just looking at it. On the room's center wall hung another 72-inch flat screen. Below the screen was a cedar bureau with several drawers and a laptop on top of it. The display screen on the laptop welcomed guests to the resort and encouraged them to check out an online list of activities the resort offered by pressing the space bar.

There were two smaller cedar bureaus on either side of the large bed. Each held a brass lamp and one housed a telephone. The room offered a private bathroom and a patio. The bathroom was decorated in black marble and brass and was equipped with a large Jacuzzi-style tub. A large glass case above the sink stored a variety of soaps, shampoos, and body oils.

"You like?" Steve asked as Tina stepped back into the bedroom.

"It's alright," she said in a lazy tone and then started laughing.

Tina took off her coat and threw it onto the bed before

making her way to the large picture window. She looked out at the white hills and tall Evergreens that seem to go on forever in every direction. In the distance, she saw people skiing and riding ski lifts. She was glad she had decided to come with Steve to the resort in Maine.

He had been very patient with her over the last few months. For a while, she had buried herself in the condo she had rented after leaving the Long Island home. She hadn't even sent for her things. She just wanted to be done with Trey and that entire situation.

Steve had kept in contact with her throughout her healing process. He always called or texted her to make sure she was alright. They had learned a lot about each other over the last several months. Now, she was ready to explore the parts of him she didn't know. It had taken her a long time to get to the point she wanted to share herself with someone. Michell and her grandmother had pushed her to get back to life. So, here she was.

Steve slipped up behind her.

"I'd love to kidnap you."

The sound of his voice caused her to feel warm and his touch was making her hot.

"I'd suffer Stockholm syndrome the second you snatched me up."

She eased away from the window and headed toward the bathroom. She needed to take a shower after their travel, even if it was only a short flight. She needed to feel totally refreshed when she gave herself over to him. After she got out the shower, he got in.

Tina tried to relax while he was in the shower. She kept checking her naked form in the mirror and wondering if he would like her body unclothed. She finally lay in the bed and waited for him. She felt like a school girl.

Her body temperature began to heat up when he appeared with a towel wrapped around his waist revealing his six-pack. Hot as she was at the moment, she needed a cold one. She reached for his tool soon as he dropped the towel to the floor. She went to work before he could even get into the bed completely.

Steve spread his knees apart on the mattress and pulled the hair back from her face as she moistened his meat with her hot tongue. She went down the length of his shaft and stroked his tool as she bounced his scrotum sac on her tongue. She worked her spit in circles on his genitals. He gripped her hair in a fist and closed his eyes and pushed his head backwards.

She looked up at him as she gobbled his nut sac up. She knew she was blowing his mind. It felt like he wasn't going to hold himself up on his knees for much longer, if she continued. She ran her tongue back up his shaft to the tip and toyed with the head of his penis with her tongue while she sucked with her jaw muscles.

He managed to position her on her side while she attacked his manhood with her tongue. He lifted up her and let his fingers find the moisture outside her love hole. He pushed one finger inside her and then another. He worked his middle and index fingers inside her, causing her to squirm and moan with pleasure as she continued to service him.

As his fingers dug inside her causing her terrible pleasure. She thought about Trey. She thought about how she never liked him to put his fingers inside her. Right here and now, she didn't mind Steve's fingers inside her one bit. She moaned aloud and rolled onto her back trying to escape the pleasure. He was on her in a flash. He had straddled her face and began to pump his organ into her hot mouth like a piston.

The vibes running over her body felt amazing. It was like her feverish state was giving her an out of body experience. She felt like she was watching herself slurp and gag on his tool. She grabbed his rod at its base with both hands to try and regain control of the situation. She wasn't really sure if she wanted more control. She was certainly happy she hadn't had any kids yet. This was definitely not one of the stories she would ever tell them.

He pulled himself free from her and crawled between her legs to her heated pussy lips. He parted her with his fingers and toyed with her clit with his tongue. When he pushed his tongue inside her it was singed by her lava-hot juices. She moaned aloud and then seemed to hum a sigh of relief as Steve explored her insides. He watched her reactions. She was on fire. Her hands ran over her breasts and her eyes were squeezed tightly shut.

He was amazing! He had lit her wick and now all the wax was melting away. She tried to call out as she released but her voice was gone, as was she. Tina reached out and grabbed the top of his head and buried it in her center as her eyes bulged.

Finally her vocal cords began to work again and she screamed out into the silence of the room, *"Gawd!"*

Steve lifted himself up from between her legs and grabbed her by the ankles. He pulled her toward the center of the bed and pushed her ankles toward her head, until her shin rest on her shoulders, and her toes touched her ears. He lifted himself up into a push-up position, balancing on his toes and palms.

His tool found her and pushed through to her boiling love hole. He drove himself full into her slowly watching the wrinkles form in her face as he touched her ends. He withdrew even slower and repeated the process three times before her muscles were relaxed enough for him to get into that rhythm he loved.

He started working his hips as he bounced inside her twirling her cream like a coffee spoon. Her moans got louder and soon she was speaking pleasurable obscenities. He felt her nails on his chest and at the small of his back every time he dug deep. Sweat dripped down his arms as he held Tina in place and really started to give it to her.

She could feel him in her stomach. He was really putting it on her now and her moans weren't enough. She screamed his name as he beat her insides like hammer and nail. She knew he was close, but she couldn't stand it any longer.

She screamed out, "Okkkay!"

He looked at her. The look on her face was pleading but he couldn't stop. He was almost there. He spread his legs further apart and started banging his body into his. Her body lifted from the mattress every time he drove himself into her. He saw the tears streaming to her ears as his nut came. He grunted and gave it all he had with one final pump. He released her feet and collapsed on top of her before rolling off to the side panting.

"Damn! That was intense! I think I'm in love," he breathed.

"Me, too."

She touched her fingers to her tears of pleasure. Finally, she'd found a man who could make her laugh and cry without ever changing her mood.

CHAPTER 18

Right Back at You…

Maze was dressed in Carhartt overalls and black Chakkas. His neck and face was covered by a thick black scarf. The red tinted ski goggles looked worn more for style rather than the weather. The dreadlocks he had fitted to his head looked authentic. Some of the locks blew in the wind that occasionally crept up blowing from the snow on the pavement. His hands were stuffed into his jacket pockets, where he also had a thirty-eight gripped in his right hand. He was waiting outside the supermarket on 149th street.

Peeto was also waiting in the warmth of the luxury Lexus sedan. Keith took his mother shopping every Saturday at noon and he was his driver/body guard/bag handler on days like today. They hadn't lived in these slums for over ten years. Keith had moved his mother out of the apartment he grew up in to a house in Yonkers. With all the dirt he was doing in the hood he couldn't afford to leave his mother at the mercy of his enemies. Still, she demanded he bring her to the grocer she knew.

Keith figured she just wanted to come to the neighborhood

week after week to see familiar faces. Peeto hated these trips to the supermarket where he was left waiting in the car for up to an hour at time. Everybody from the hood watched him put groceries into the trunk when they finally emerged from the supermarket. He was posted like some type of sentry.

It wasn't so bad in the summer when the young girls would be cruising up and down the street in tight-fitting Daisy Dukes and halter tops but in the cold there was nothing to do except listen to the radio and wait.

Peeto peered at his watch. Thirty-five minutes had gone by. He looked out the window and saw the same Negro with dreadlocks and a scarf over his face before going back to turning the radio dial. A song from the Hustle Kingz came on and he thought about the robbery they had committed. They had killed one of the dudes associated with the group. That's what these fake gangsters get for coming back to the hood. Had he not been so caught up in his thoughts, Peeto may have been more concerned about the black dude bundled up bopping his head.

Mrs. Douglas, at seventy, bickered with the energy of a nest full of newborn robins. Keith couldn't wait for the cashier to scan the last few items and put them into a bag. He quickly loaded the cart causing his mother to scold him for crushing her bread with the milk. He adjusted the items and began pushing the cart toward the exit with his mother quick on his heels. He swiped a fresh peach from the fruit stand as he went by.

Keith bit into the peach and savored it's sweetness as he pushed the cart through the long strips of plastic that led from the produce section to the street. He was set to take another bite when a figure in all black and dreadlocks appeared holding a gun pointed at him. He briefly saw his own reflection in the red tint of the gunman's ski goggles before the first shot tore through his throat and he collapsed unable to breathe and choking on his own blood.

He looked shocked as he lay dying wishing he had enough air to warn his mother to get back inside the supermarket. It was too late. She appeared in the doorway just as the gunman stepped over him and put another slug in the middle of his forehead. Mrs. Douglas screamed when she saw the gunman standing over her son. The gunman wasted no time by silencing her with a shot to the face. The slug lifted her frail frame off the ground and threw her violently back through the plastic.

Peeto had just reached for the radio dial again when he heard the first shot. When he looked through the car window, he saw the dude with the dreadlocks standing over Keith. He saw the flash from the muzzle and then he saw it again as the gunman shot Mrs. Douglas. Peeto reached for the door handle rushing to get out of the car. As he did, Maze turned around with a wicked smile on his face and shot through the passenger side window of the car. The bullet hit Peeto in the thigh spinning him off balance.

Peeto dropped the nine millimeter he had been clutching. Maze ran around the car and squeezed two more shots into Peeto's face leaving him dead in the street between the open door and the car's interior. Maze looked around quickly before spinning away.

*****

Holmes and Miller had just come from meeting with an informant. Miller was as excited as could be. The information they had just received was surely enough to shut down their favorite crew from over at Global Entertainment. He couldn't wait to get back to headquarters and make out the warrants. The first person he was going to pick up was Trey.

"I think we should sit on this thing for a while. See what's going to happen with the other thing," Holmes said as he turned into the headquarters parking lot.

Miller snapped his neck around to look at him. He couldn't believe what he was hearing.

"What the hell do you mean? We got enough to go forward right now. Fuck the other thing. We don't even know if that shit's going to happen."

"You sound more eager than a fan with a pair of concert tickets. What have we been doing here?"

"Building a case and, now, we finally got one. And, our informant is solid. This ain't no groupie or somebody they used to employ. This is the fuckin' messenger man!"

"I hear you but remember we haven't just been running around chasing these fools. We've been putting in a lot of hours on the other case, too. If our informant is right, if not, we'll just go with what we know. We can just close both cases at once. You get what I'm saying."

A smile crept to Millers' lips, "I know exactly what you're saying, my man."

Miller reached over and gave Holmes some dap.

"Man, for a minute you had me thinking you were getting off the Mic," Miller chuckled.

The Mic was what they called the unit they worked out of. All the cops in the unit had emcee pseudonyms as well.

"And, go back to pushing a regular squad car? Shit, I don't ride on nothing less than twenties, my nigga."

The two detectives laughed as they got out of the Hummer.

Chapter 19

Black on Both Sides

Dana tapped her pen on her desk. She looked at Skarz sitting across from her, her trusty comrade no matter what. The industry tabloids had tried to shame her for her false claims of being pregnant by Trey. Her doctor's official medical records and the false document she had manufactured had surfaced on MTV and the internet. From there, the story took a life of its own.

She had started in radio so she knew how to play the situation. She just stayed low. When she did attend industry functions where media was going to be present, she knew how to handle them. The label was doing well and no one could argue that. That became her spin. Scandal could never outrun success in a long distance race but it had been a personal embarrassment to her. She wanted to get even with Trey. He had betrayed her after she had made him, just like Scheme. Now, it was time for him to pay, just like Scheme.

A smile crept to her lips as she thought about that night so long ago. It had started earlier in the evening with Skarz and her in an office not quite as big as this one. She had decided to kill Scheme and Crystal, but she had to set it up just right. That night at the club when the fight broke out, she knew it was time to act.

They had all been back stage waiting for Scheme to go on. Dana had been in a serious stare down with Crystal. She had told Scheme earlier that day that he would have to move out the label's house within 90 days. He must have told Crystal because soon as she had walked into his dressing room, she had confronted her.

"So, you want me out the house? Don't be a sore loser, bitch!" Crystal spat.

Skarz had stepped between the women. Crystal stood on the other side of the room seething when they heard a loud commotion out in the hallway. When Skarz opened the door he saw a bunch of guys fighting with each other and security. Just as he was closing the door, one kid slashed another across the face with a razor. He quickly closed and locked the door.

"Yo, we gotta get the hell out of here. They're tearing the place apart out there."

"What the hell happened?" Scheme asked.

"How the fuck am I supposed to know? I'm in here with you." Skarz said as he pulled his gun from its holster.

Big Jay, the promoter, came through another door in the dressing room and told them to follow him. He led them through a maze of back doors and exits until they came out in an alley in back of the club.

"What the hell happened in there?" Scheme asked Jay.

"I don't know, man. This dude was on the stage killin' shit and the next thing you know a fight breaks out backstage and shit went bananas. Look. Y'all good. Just walk down that way and y'all will come out in the front. Dana, I'll call you tomorrow. We'll fix this. I gotta go find this kid and give him his money."

"You better find me tomorrow and give me mines," Dana said.

"I got you, Dana Dane. We'll work something out."

"Hells yeah, we will. That shit was packed in there and they didn't come to see the kid who was killin' shit. They came to see Scheme."

"Dana, I got you. Let me get back in here before they tear the club up and everybody lose money."

They walked down the alley to the front of the club. People were still filing out and some people were still shouting and creating small disturbances.

"Where you parked at?" Dana asked Scheme.

"I'm down the block in a garage. Where you at?"

"I'm in a cab. You know I don't park my shit in Brooklyn nowhere, garage or no garage. Skarz go with them and make sure they get home safe."

"We good," Scheme said.

"No you're not good. You got L.A. next week. I can't afford for nothing to happen to you. Skarz is going to be your chauffer and body guard tonight. I gotta protect my investment. You and Miss Homemaker from the projects have a good evening."

Dana stepped into the street and hailed a cab. Skarz restrained Crystal from going after her.

"Fuck you, bitch!" Crystal screamed.

Dana pulled open the cab door, got in, and rolled down the window.

"No, boo boo, fuck with me."

She rolled the window back up and the cab drove off. She knew Skarz would handle the rest and he had. Now, it was time for him to go to work again. Dana dropped the pen on her desk, plucked three red grapes from the stem, and grabbed a slice of hot cheese. She chewed the cheese and grapes thinking of the best way for Trey to die. Shooting him was too simple.

"Skarz."

He looked up from his Kindle.

"Get your head out the books. Once again, it's on."

"You got a new scheme?"

"A better scheme," she corrected.

CHAPTER 20

I Know You Seen Me in the Video

The club was dark. Special lighting effects showed splashes of burgundy on the walls. Black linen covered the tables with a black candle burning on each. Smoke crept along the floor. A pair of legs appeared stepping right in front of left with sophisticated strides. Next were the thighs and the crotch, the flat stomach and the full cleavage. Annie appeared in full screen.

She was flailing her arms, bopping her head, and poking her index fingers at the camera. She was wearing a three quarter yellow Chinchilla coat, her matching bikini her puffy camel toe was partially hidden behind the *A* and *O* in diamonds. Her hair was dyed yellow and her Cuban link with the Jesus piece was Canary yellow. The camera man eased out the shot as she began her rap.

"Lust of the world, juicy pussy holster girl/ sick wit' my shit you suppose to earl/ The breast behind the ski-mask consider this the peep show/ The pump jump in my hands, make ya brains skeet, yo"

Trey appeared out of the shadows and put a hand over Annie's mouth as she mouthed the word 'skeet'. Then, just like that, he faded back into the darkness.

"Run in ya house guns drawn, want the drugs and the chips/Any signs of hesitation then I'm pluggin' ya bitch/ Gun buttin' the kid, yo the niggas I'm wit'…/Will leave everybody shot and the furniture flipped."

"Alright good. Cut!" the director screamed.

Annie looked around and saw Trey standing in a corner alone. She walked over to him.

"What up, Trey? You been acting funny lately. You a'ight?"

"Yeah. I'm good, Annie. It's just not fun no more."

"What?"

"Nothing."

Annie pushed his shoulder.

"Knock it off this me you talking to."

"Shit, just crazy right now. I'm missing Tina. I feeling like I'm falling out of love with hip-hop. This shit just a job now. I lost me in this shit, but I gained a piece of life. Look, no more cup. I'm sweeping up my yard. I'm ready to walk away after I give your aunt this last album. You were right that day long ago at the radio station. I understand now."

"Is this nigga over here giving you a sermon on how he's thinkin' bout retiring" Boogs asked as he walked up to them.

"He don't believe me because we," Trey waved his hand between him and Boogs. "He don't think I can do it."

"I know you can't, nigga. But, I came to holla at you on some other shit real quick before we start shootin' again."

"What's up?"

"You can stop moping around. That shit wit Fogg is handled."

"I read about a situation in the paper."

Boogs smiled, "Yup."

"Son, what are you doing? You have to slow down so you can really find yourself."

Boogs looked at Annie and pointed at Trey.

"Here he go again. What do you mean? What I'm doin'? I'm looking out for our family! You think you too big to love ya niggas?"

"I love you all. We just live different now. The goal we had together we accomplished that. Now, we're at a fork in the road. It may be time we go in separate directions."

"I gotta keep in mind you buggin' cause you thinkin' 'bout Tina. You need to get over that, man."

"I'm going to get over a lot of things. I'm changing."

Boogs looked at Trey and shook his head. He tapped Maze who was standing next to him. "Son trippin'. Let's go. Annie, talk some sense into my man."

Boogs walked off shaking his head with Maze walking at his side. Annie looked at Trey. She touched a palm to his shoulder.

"I told you what it was. This shit will eat you alive if you let it. I see you changing but staying drug free can't take the needle with the dope out of your arm long as you keep walking around the devil's advocates. Remember what you told me after your grandfather's funeral? You said you weren't sad. He had died a dope fiend. 'Cause dope was what made him most happy. It's the gift and the curse. If you quit, you'll feel like you're dying. If you keep it up, it will kill you for sure. Come on. We gotta go to the next location so you can get your verse in. Cheer up. You the best rapper alive."

He watched her go. He thought about what she had just said. She was right. Some of his fondest memories of his grandfather were when he was on dope. Music was his dope. He couldn't escape the gift God had given him, this talent but this heroin stamped fame, was the worst kind of dope. It can take you to heaven while dragging you through hell. The same ones that lift their glasses to toast your presence will be the same ones that will frown on you when you when you're holding a cup.

He knew deep down he couldn't quit. He wasn't going to quit. He had gone to see his mother after he realized Tina really had moved on. She was so happy to see him. He had been writing and sending money but he hadn't gone to see her before.

She was that same strong woman he had remembered. She took his face in her hands and wiped away his tears. She apologized for not being there for his first heart break. Then, she kept it a thousand with him.

She looked him in his eyes and told him all the things he had done to break his own heart by breaking a woman who loved him. It was amazing how well she knew him. Her perception of him as her son and a star were dead on. Despite all the years she had been away, she still knew her child.

His moment of clarity came then. He knew he had to separate himself from the people in his life so he could truly become great at being who he was. He was going to leave World Domination after they fulfilled the contract. He was going to going to mend things with Tina, their friendship. At least they were on speaking terms now.

He was going to see if she would get him in over to A.B.J. and handle the direction of his solo project. She had gotten an executive position over there, and she had offered help the last time they bumped into each other. She looked happy and he was happy for her. She deserved it. Like his mother said, he used to love her so he should understand why someone else would, too. Yeah, Trey used to love her and he always would.

Chapter 21

Hot Damn Ho'

Skarz pushed his face further into the pillow, almost suffocating himself trying to muffle his screams. He felt his penis began to jerk and squirt his pleasure onto the mattress. He let out a sigh of relief as the spear withdrew from his rectum. He felt the softness of the palm as it smacked his buttocks.

"All done, baby. Momma does it again!"

He pulled his face from the pillow and rolled onto his back. He watched as Annie removed the strap-on. Her body was perfect. He wished he had her ass, her breasts. There wasn't a doctor on earth that could carve out her structure. The girl had definitely been touched by God's hands.

Their sexual romps had started years ago when he had been responsible for running her around to different meetings and the studio. Everyone wanted to meet the young girl with the gorgeous body. He had felt bad taking her around knowing Dana basically had been pimping her out to get her an album deal, a deal that Dana ultimately got rich off and Annie nibbled from the crumbs.

He had exposed his sexual preference to her as a means

of soothing her character. He had offered to let her fuck him for his own guilty pleasures.

"Girl, you are amazing."

"You think so?" she said smiling as she gathered her things to go to the shower.

"You already know. Your aunt is tripping again."

"What do you mean?"

She paused at the entrance to the bathroom and gave him a look as he lay toying with his flaccid penis.

"She's become fixated on Trey. Another one of her Erica Kane moments where she wants to destroy everything she created and the things she didn't create."

"Oh, Gawd. What? Is she still upset about the pregnancy thing? She accomplished her goal. Trey's not with Tina anymore."

"Yeah about that..." he sat up.

"I don't think she can live down that Tina put the Swizz Beats on her in the precinct."

"Child boo, Dana ain't never been known as a fighter. That ain't nothing to live down," Annie said with a wave of her hand.

"I just saw Tina last week at BUTCH's album release. She didn't mention Trey or Dana. That girl was there with her new man and she got her life."

"Well, you know your aunt better than anybody."

"I do though. So, what you gonna do?"

"What I always do. Make the queen happy even when I don't like her rule."

"If you keep playing a jester in the queen's ballroom, the joke's gonna end up on you. Be careful is all I can say."

"That's the same thing you said to me about Scheme and I'm still here and he's gone. Don't worry. I'm sure your aunt has somebody to pen your next album for you."

"That's the thing. Y'all stay scheming. I got one more hit in me, but I'm going to write it myself. No more crutches. It's time I give the people the real Annie."

"Are you gonna tell them about this," he said smiling.

"That's gonna be the first thing I tell 'em. I might even throw you a couple dollars,"

She laughed and walked into the bathroom.

"Well, let me be your cover model."

He yelled at the bathroom door before chuckling to himself.

"Cover model," he said again to himself as he heard the shower water start to run.

Annie stepped under the steaming hot water. She thought about her life as the water beat against her body. She thought about how she had run away from home and no one had even come looking for her.

She wondered if her mother ever saw her on TV and recognized her. Probably not. She probably never wanted to see her face again. She had told her that night to get out of her house and never come back.

Her mother's boyfriend, Roy, had been sexually abusing her for years. She had never said a word. That last time she had been cramping something terrible. Roy wouldn't listen. So, she smacked him across the face. He beat her like she was a grown man before raping her. He raped her all night while her mother was at work. He only stopped because it was time for him to go to work.

When her mother had come home she had found her right where Roy had left her beaten and in pain. Her mother had run to her franticly asking her what had happened. When she told her Roy had beaten and raped her, her mother's attitude changed completely. Annie was no longer a victim. She was no longer her daughter.

Annie sometimes dreamed she would get a call saying that her birth mother had been looking for her. She would go to wherever she was and fall into her arms. She would forgive her because she now understood how hard it was to be a woman and how easy it was to be a victim.

Annie turned the water off and got out of the shower drying her tears first.

CHAPTER 22

The Message

Boogs got the call he had been waiting on for months now. Candice, the stripper who knew Anonymous, had called earlier and told him that Anonymous would be coming by the club later that night. Boogs immediately called Maze. He planned to show him he wasn't no studio gangster but was a true to life G tonight.

He hadn't even called his wild cousins from Brooklyn in on this one. They had decided against telling Bigga what was set to go down, too. He wanted them to pull this mission off on their own. He really wanted to be involved in the hit so when he talked to Smurf he could give him intimate details.

He went to retrieve his gun from its box and paced the room. Every few seconds he would lift the gun at imaginary targets and pretend to pull the trigger. He felt a surge of power as he held the gun in his hand. He stopped pacing and studied the piece of steel in his hand. He pulled the slide back and cocked it, before tucking it in his waistline.

He met Maze near Lincoln projects and drove to 125th street. He parked across from the after-hours strip joint and waited. Candace was supposed to call him when they were on their way out. He pulled the gun from his waist and looked at it.

Maze looked over at him. "You ready nigga?"

"I'm definitely ready."

"Okay, my nigga. You take care of him and his man and I'll take care of the chicks."

Boogs looked over at him.

"What nigga? You thought we was gonna leave witnesses. The bitch know you. Smarten up, my dude. You sure you ready for this? This ain't the booth, nigga. You ain't bout to spit a hot sixteen. You 'bout to put a nigga down. Man, just don't get sick in the car after shit is over."

"Man, fuck you. I got this!"

"A'ight."

The two men stopped talking and sat waiting for the call.

*****

The club was a dimly lit, smoked-fill pool of sexual activity. Strippers walked around totally nude offering sexual favors for cash and taking offers for the right price. Two women performed sixty-nine for a small group of men who were throwing twenties, fifties, and hundreds at them as they devoured each other. A Spanish female was bent at the waist with her face on the table stuffed in a mound of coke. Fooquan spread her buttocks and licked her ass and pussy.

Anonymous had his face stuffed into Candice's pussy as she lay on her back on one of the round tables. He was eating her out really well. He slurped at her juices as they dripped from his lips to his chin. Her home girl, Coco, was giving him head beneath the table as he feasted on Candace. Candice pulled his face away from her dripping center by tugging the curls of his afro causing him to look at her.

She nibbled on her bottom lip and moistened it with her tongue before she spoke, "You want me and my girl together? I got somebody special for your friend, too."

Anonymous could hardly answer because Coco was doing such a number on him under the table. He just grunted and shook his head yes.

"Not here doe. We going to head to her spot or get a room. The manager of the club, gonna want a piece of the action if we go to the rooms in the back. I ain't tryin' to be giving up no paper. I'm already givin' up the pussy," Candice said still tugging at his curls.

"Let us get our shit and meet us outside."

She finally let go of the curls and rolled from the table to her feet. Coco was right on queue coming from under the table following her back to the dressing room.

Anonymous and Fooquan took a few minutes to get themselves together before heading toward the door. Back in the dressing room, Candice and Coco ran wipes between their legs and thighs. Candice got out her phone and dialed Boogs' number.

"I'm on my way," she said and hung up.

Candice quickly dressed. Candice, Coco, and the Spanish girl made their way to the door where Anonymous and his friend were waiting anxiously.

As soon as the five of them reached the street, they set off in the direction of Anonymous' truck. As they reached the SUV, Boogs stepped into view from the rear of the truck.

"Yo, yo, Anonymous!"

Anonymous turned to see who was calling him and saw Boogs pointing at the white T-shirt he wore. The letters on it read STOP SNITCHING. Boogs lifted his P-89 pistol as Fooquan reached for his waistline. Boogs fired two shots into his chest that lifted Fooquan off his feet and slammed him to the ground. Anonymous pulled the truck's door open but that was as far as he got before Boogs pumped four slugs into him leaving him slumped across the SUV's seat.

The three girls' screamed and started trying to ease away when Maze slipped up behind them, and let loose with a Mac-11. The shots caused the girl's' bodies to dance until he let up off the trigger. The three of them fell to the pavement. He pumped two more shells in Candice's face and three more into her body because her finger was twitching.

They tucked the guns as they started back across the street to the Astro van they had drove. Police came from every direction with guns drawn. Before Maze and Boogs could react, they were snatched from the van and thrown to the pavement.

When they were put into restraints and lifted to their feet, Boogs saw Miller and Holmes. He knew the two dicks had been following them around. They had even seen them out of state when they were doing shows. He had never had any contact with them but Trey had. He dropped his head as Miller began reading him his rights.

During the trip to the precinct, Boogs struggled to come to grips with the fact that his man had set him up. The one thing he couldn't figure was how he knew. Trey hadn't been coming around much. They mostly met at the studio to work on their second album. He knew he was going through a change and all, but he would have never thought it was this deep. All his preaching and bible talk in the studio had led to him confessing.

When they got Boogs and Maze to the precinct, they kept them separated. It wasn't until Maze was brought into a room where there was a chart with almost everyone from the label's face on it. He studied the chart. That's when he knew that his homie hadn't told on him but he knew who had.

G STREET CHRONICLES
A LITERARY POWERHOUSE
WWW.GSTREETCHRONICLES.COM

CHAPTER 23

It All Falls Down

"I'm on point to you like an Irish setter. You'll get none of my chips/ I got ya picture framed wanted for dicks, that's all you good for is fuckin' my pits/ I'm tough on a bitch cause so many ho's be scheming swallow this semen/ I can't afford no baby screamin'…"

Dana picked up the remote and rewound the video. She listened again then she turned the TV off. Trey had dissed her on a record called Million Dollar Pussy, featuring her niece. They had even hired a look alike for the video. She hadn't had time to look at the preview copy the network had sent her over. She heard and saw it for the first time with everyone else during its world premiere.

She thought about turning her phone back on just to see who was going to start blowing her phone. She'd check her messages in the morning. Annie had never mentioned that Trey had changed his verse on the song. That definitely wasn't the album version. She wasn't worried. She'd have the video pulled in a few days and she'd release the song as a single while people were buzzing over the video's disappearance. If they think the song is about her let them buy the single. Besides, their look-alike did her no justice. She had to find out who she was and make sure never entered another music video set again.

She wondered where Skarz was. He was supposed to have been here when she got home. It was getting late. She'd talk to him in the morning. She had finally figured out how they were going to get rid of Trey. She picked up her phone and turned off the lights in the living room. She had a big day tomorrow. It was time to see if Paul was going to approve her new budget plan.

Dana stopped and stood still in the darkness of the hallway that led to the stairs. She thought she heard something. She listened but heard nothing. She started toward the stairs. When her foot hit the first step she was grabbed from behind.

A hand covered her mouth so she couldn't scream. The strong grip held her firmly preventing her from escaping. She kicked her legs and struggled as she was dragged toward the living room.

Her attacker put her in a sleeper hold and whispered into her ear, "Do you want to die?"

Dana shook her head. Tears ran down her face. She had no idea who it was and how he'd had gotten into her house. Where was Skarz? Her mind was racing a mile a minute and her heart was beating even faster. Had Trey found out about their plot to kill him and sent someone to kill her? She prayed silently that whoever this was wouldn't kill her. She felt a prick in her neck and then her body started feeling numb before she went limp in her captor's arms. She was fading. Fading, fading…

Miller and Holmes had the swat team set up a perimeter all around Dana's house. She had a lot of land and they didn't want to take any chances of her slipping away from them. It was also the reason they had come to get her right after they had taken Boogs and Maze into custody. She was a flight risk if they didn't get her into custody quickly. It had already been a media circus when they arrested Boogs.

Miller and Holmes were hidden from view in the tree line right at the edge of her property with the rest of the tactical response team. They thought her bodyguard might be inside with her but they weren't sure. They had a warrant for his arrest as well. If he was there, it would save them the trouble of looking for him later.

Teams were set up around Trey and Bigga as well. They would execute their warrants the moment they radioed in that they had the mother goose in custody. Right now, they were just waiting to get a chopper out here so they could have air cover if there was a pursuit. They doubted anyone would get far with all the dogs and men they had on the ground, but hey you could never be sure.

Inside the house Dana woke up with a pounding head ache. She was stripped nude and her body was face down, ass up over the arm of her sofa. Her hands were cuffed behind her back, and all the feeling hadn't returned to her legs yet, so she didn't know if they had restraints on them too. She smelled an awful smell.

She heard footsteps behind her then she saw the white man with the thick bi-focal glasses. She had seen him somewhere before, but she couldn't recall where.

"What do you want?" she managed to ask weakly.

"Me. I want to have some fun. I like to experiment, try new things. Do you like to experiment, Dana?"

Oh, God, he was going to rape her. She shook her head no.

"Too bad. See, I love to experiment. I love it so much and do it so often that some people say I'm disturbed. But they just don't understand talent. You understand talent. Don't you, Dana?"

Who was this guy? She knew she was going to die if she didn't think of something fast.

"Please, I have money."

"I know you have money, Dana. I don't want your money. I told you I want to experiment. I bet you're wondering what that God awful smell is. I used your kitchen I hope you don't mind. What you smell, Dana, is raw lard. No processing or nothing, right off the pig. I been boiling it for a minute. I think it's ready. Does it smell ready to you? Aww you've probably never even had raw boiled lard. How would you know what it smells like? I'll be right back, Dana. Excuse me for a moment."

Dana tried to lift her body up when she heard him walk out of the living room, but there was no use. Whatever he had shot her with had paralyzed her from the neck down. This was crazy like a scene right out of the movies. He even had a calm, creepy voice every time he said her name. She closed her eyes and prayed some more. She heard him returning.

She felt the pressure of his hand slapping her numb buttocks. Then, he appeared before her holding a turkey baster with a hideous look gray substance in it.

"Did I ever tell you I love your ass, Dana? Your niece has a nice ass, too. To keep it a hundred with you. Did I say that right?"

He looked at her with a crazy smile.

"I've always wondered what a real lard ass would look like so today. I'm going to see."

He walked behind her and parted her buttocks he saw the pink from her pussy peeping at him. He poked a finger inside her and she jerked a little. He then stuck his finger in her anal cavity. He pulled it out and put it in his mouth and sucked on it.

"You know, Dana. You need to wash your ass better and your pussy's dry but, shit, you're probably not as excited as me. I get it. Now, this is gonna burn a little 'cause this stuff is piping hot. Why you think I got the metal baster? Any who. Scream if you love it."

"He parted her buttocks again and eased the tip of the baster into her rectum. He pushed it a quarter of the way then withdrew it. He could see her squirming from the feel of the heat. He put the baster back inside her and went a little deeper this time. He heard her breathing hard. He gripped the small cushion at the top of the baster and squeezed it as he shoved the baster further. The hot lard released from the tube and Dana screamed like nobody's tomorrow.

He pulled the baster out and watched as the lard leaked from her rectum. He took a step back and clapped his hands appreciatively.

"Oh my, I gotta get a picture of this. Wait here. Let me get my camera phone. You have to see this. The skin around your rectum maybe a little singed but, hey, you were dark already."

Miller heard a scream come from the house and radioed his inner perimeter guys to see if they had breached the house. They had responded no. He looked at Holmes, jumped up and took off running toward the house. The rest of the tactical team followed his lead. When he reached the front door he kicked it in and flanked to his left. He encountered a startled-looking white man with a camera phone. Before he could direct the man to stand clear, he saw him reach for his waist and come out with a pistol.

Miller fired two quick rounds into the guy's chest. The

suspect dropped the gun and fell to the floor hard. The rest of the team rushed the room and that's when Miller saw Dana. She was a pitiful sight. Her anal cavity looked like it had been torched. The team cleared the rest of the house. They found Skarz in a closet in the basement with a twenty-two bullet in his head.

Miller called the other teams and told them to hit their target mother goose was in custody. Then, he called for EMS and the coroner.

Chapter 24

It Was Written

When the Hip-Hop Task Force kicked in Trey's door and dragged him out of his home he wasn't worried. He wasn't worried when they told him he was being arrested for murder and conspiracy. He wasn't worried until he was placed in an interrogation room and Miller poked his head in.

"I told you I'd see you later, rapper. We got your girl, too. She's at the hospital. She's messed up real bad."

He was worried now. What girl? Who was he talking about? Dana? Annie? Tina?

What the hell was going on? He got up and banged on the door. He couldn't believe it when Cory walked in with a badge around his neck.

Trey laughed. "Get the fuck outta here. You Five-O, man? This shit crazy. What I'm doing here?"

"You're being charged with murder for the deaths of Anonymous, Fooquan, Keith Douglas and his mother-"

"Who are these people? Man, you fuckin' trippin'. Anonymous is dead?"

"Yup. Sure is. He died on the scene. We caught your boys

red-handed."

"What boys? What are you talkin' 'bout for real? I need my lawyer."

"Okay. Well, this conversation is over but before you call your lawyer you might wanna rap with me. We got a witness. She knows everything. You know her well, too, Annie Oakley."

"Bullshit. Get me a phone pig so I can call my lawyer and get up out of here."

Cory looked at him and laughed.

"Who you fronting for, Trey? It's me and you baby. Remember you a gangsta rapper, not a gangster. Shit to keep it real with you homie. I don't even think you're that good of a rapper. You was just a means to an end. Whoever came through that studio that Dana liked was gonna be the next star."

Cory smirked.

"You think you one of a kind dude? There's a million yous out there in those boroughs. We were trying to get Dana for Scheme. We missed her on that. But we got you." Cory walked out the room leaving Trey sitting there stunned.

Annie had been working with Cory for almost a year and a half. She had been busted on one of Dana's money runs and he told her he was with the Hip Hop task force. He had originally been assigned to investigate the Scheme homicide, but when he got inside and saw what was going on he started going at the case from another angle.

Trey couldn't believe it, wouldn't believe it, until he was arraigned in federal court two days later. He stood between Boogs and Maze as the judge read the charges against him and the others.

He had nothing to do with those murders any of them.

He had been hurt when Fogg was killed, He had been angry but he didn't plot to kill Keith and his mother. He didn't like Anonymous, but he hadn't sat with them and said let's knock this guy off. He was a rapper. He was Jarod Duffy.

After their arraignment, they were remanded to federal custody with no bail. Dana and Bigga had been indicted on wire fraud charges and were both facing up to thirty years. Bigga had also been indicted on drug distribution charges that could get him life.

The cops knew things Trey hadn't even known were going on like about the money being transferred on the tour buses and the whole network Dana had set up to wash the money including the phony companies and the phony accounts. He had been oblivious but the feds knew it all.

He was being held because Annie had said he had been present at certain conversation where the murders were mentioned. The attorney general's office ran with that. Even after she made a sworn deposition and said she had never heard him say anything about killing anyone he was still indicted.

As sour as he felt, Dana had to feel worst. She had been betrayed by someone she had taken in. She had spent the first six months of her incarceration in the jail infirmary. She had eventually taken a deal for twenty years and had forfeited all of her assets, at least, all that they knew about. Trey knew Dana hadn't given it all up. She would have had something stashed.

It was often said you couldn't buy loyalty and Bigga had found out in the worst way. After he was locked up, he had no more influence or money on the streets. Anybody who owed him just deaded him. What was he going do? He was looking at life. He couldn't even pay for a lawyer.

He'd gotten slammed with forty years.

Boogs had got the best deal his high priced attorney could work out. A sweet deal is what they had called it. He would have to serve a minimum of 360 months followed by a lifetime of parole.

Maze took life without the possibility of parole in order to avoid the death penalty. At the end of the day, he wasn't as gangster as he thought. He didn't want to die. He had just wanted to kill. His gangster persona was reduced to a number and head count every few hours for the rest of his life.

Trey thought about Maze most because that was the same sentence he was facing. He had been sitting in this cell for the last fifteen months thinking about that. It was coming down to the moment of truth. The jury had his case. He was waiting for a verdict. His lawyer urged him to be patient. The more the jury considered the facts the better it would be for him. A quick jury usually meant certain death. They had been deliberating for two days.

Trey thought about his mother. He needed her strength but he couldn't communicate with her. The feds didn't allow inmate to inmate correspondence.

He couldn't even walk out into the jail's population because he was such a high profile inmate due to his celebrity. He didn't feel like a celebrity when he listened to the radio. They would play some of the Hustle Kingz' old hits, but he mostly heard new artist. The streets were saying some rapper named C-Sharp was the new king of rap.

They hadn't forgotten him but he had been replaced quickly. Fame really was fifteen minutes. It just felt like a lifetime if you became your own fan. Trey heard a guard coming down the corridor.

He stopped at his cell and said, "Get yourself together.

You're going over to the court. They got a verdict."

Trey's his heart fluttered. He put on his court clothes and got on his knees to pray. When the guard came back to get him, he was prepared. Trey was lead through a sea of paparazzi. He saw The Geek. It was the first time he had seen him since being locked up.

He nodded and winked as Trey was escorted down the hall. As he entered the courtroom, his eyes swept the benches. They were filled with people some wearing Hustle Kingz and Trey-Eight tees. The one person he had hoped to see hadn't showed up for one day of his trial. Tina was not among the faces that stared at him as he walked in the courtroom.

Tina had sent him a card and said she was praying for him. He had written her a letter, but she had never responded. Camecca and Fahkira had come to visit him often since he had been incarcerated. That was how he had found out that Tina was pregnant.

Trey had been hurt, but he was happy for her. He had still held out hope that she would come to the courthouse for the verdict. He wanted to see her one last time. It cut him deeply to know that she didn't want to see him.

Trey walked to defendant's table and sat next to his attorney. He felt the butterflies active in his stomach again. His lawyer leaned close to him.

"Where just waiting for the judge to come in and bring the jury back in to read the verdict. How you feel?"

"I guess I'm as good as I'll ever be. There's no turning back now."

"I think we made a good case. They don't have you planning anything by their own witness's testimony. I think the girl, Annie, hurt them more than she helped them in your case. Were you guy's friends before this?"

"We were cool. We had an understanding."

"Don't worry. I like this jury."

Trey just shook his head. He thought about Annie and the last time they saw each other. She hadn't let on anything was wrong. She had been in the studio with him while he was recording the verse where he was dissing Dana; cheering him on. She really had this show biz thing down pat. She had played her role better than all of them.

The judge entered the courtroom and everyone stood up. After everyone was seated, he had the court officer bring the jury in. Trey could read a sign from one face as they filled the jury box.

"I understand the jury has reached a verdict?" the judge asked looking to the foreman.

"We have, Your Honor."

The bailiff went to retrieve the verdict and handed the slip of paper to the judge. The judge unfolded the paper looked at it and then looked at the defendant's table. Trey felt his heart sink.

"Will the defendant stand?" the judge said.

He had called him *defendant.* Trey felt weak as he got to his feet. The judge started reading but all he heard was music. He heard the many songs he had recorded and the songs he would never record.

Trey didn't realize the jury had found him not guilty until his lawyer took him in his arms and hugged him. There was a deafening echo of applause as the judge beat his gavel in an effort to restore order.

Tina watched Trey walked down the court steps with his lawyer and The Geek. He was surrounded by his fans. She turned off the TV. She was happy for him. She had no doubts he would be back on top in no time. She thought about something her mother had once said: Sometimes the time you spend apart from a person trying to make it work, will be the blessing to show you were you really need to be. She finally understood now.

She walked in the dayroom and looked at her daughter, Sparkle, sleeping peacefully in the bassinette. She looked like her father. She smiled, and made a silent prayer that she never wanted to be a star.

Chapter 25

Than to Never Have Loved at All

Dana stared at Trey on the cover of Hip Hop Weekly. He was sitting on a throne. On his head was an old antique crown with a crack in it. The camera man had caught his profile on the side of his face where he had been slashed. The caption read *Long Live the King!*

The article inside told about his partnership with Global chairman Paul Lanno to run his own label. She wasn't bitter. He was free. He was rich and successful. Another one of her stars was shining. She'd see him again.

Her lawyer had already started working on getting her sentence restructured. She would be out in about thirty six months if everything moved along as her lawyer had said they would.

She was still on top of her game. She had four million stashed away in an offshore account under her mother's name. It was a precaution she had taken at the beginning of her little money laundering business. It turned out to be a saving grace. She never thought her mother would be there for her like she had been there for Annie. It was funny how Karma worked.

She realized at that moment there was no right or wrong. Just a play; either you made the play or you got out the game. She had already suited up. She planned to play to the buzzer.

Dana set the magazine down on her desk and picked up her bag of red grapes. She popped three grapes into her mouth and closed her eyes. A smile crept across her lips. She thought about the expensive wines she had tasted over the years. Soon, she would have her life back.

"Hey, girl, what you in here doing? Dreaming 'bout that fab life you going to return to?"

Dana opened her eyes and saw her friend Redd. One of the few women she spoke to in the prison. She had been a queen pin in the dope game. She had been in for almost fourteen years. She liked her. She had shown her the ropes when she first got here and helped her cope.

"Yeah, girl. I know you told me to stop trying to bring the world in here and think about getting out of here. But, girl, when you lived how I lived, it's kinda hard to just forget. It's a little different from the dope game."

"I hear you, girl. I just stopped by to tell you I got a letter from my son today."

"Awww, girl, that's good. He finally wrote you. I know you're happy."

"Yup. He sent a picture, too."

"Oh, girl, let me see."

Redd walked into the cell and pulled a picture from her shirt pocket and threw it on top of the magazine. Dana picked the picture up and looked at it. Redd was wearing a long sable coat and a little boy was holding onto her leg. She wondered why he hadn't sent a recent picture.

"Aww, girl, he's precious. You'll get back out there to

him," Dana said throwing three more grapes into her mouth.

Redd took the picture and put it back in her shirt pocket. She pulled a shank from her waistline.

"Maybe. But you'll never get back out there to him."

Dana tried to spit the grapes out of her mouth and scream, but it was too late. Redd pushed the shank through her neck. Her eyes rolled into the back of her head as her body fell to the cell floor. Redd watched as her body twitched and blood ran from her mouth with the grapes. She picked up the magazine and left the cell.

*****

Paul Lanno lay in the bed looking up at the ceiling. He had dodged a bullet when Gregory had been killed by police at Dana's house. They figured he was a deranged home invader. They actually used the incident in the media to say they had saved Dana's life. They had.

When Annie had showed up at the office two days ago with pictures of the security guard from the studio with that deranged smile hugging her waist, Paul knew he had a new problem to deal with.

Dana was good, but Annie was amazing. They had just struck a deal that neither one of them could refuse. She was about to take over Dana's position at the label. She planned to rename the company Co-Conspirators Entertainment group. He looked over at the paperwork and his signature stamp on the desk. The deal had cost him ten million dollars. The police had no clue that Gregory was, but Annie had figured out who he was. She had figured out a lot.

Paul sat up in the bed twisting his ring. He looked at Annie as she stood on the balcony. He pulled the covers back and walked out to the balcony. His flaccid penis came to life as he looked at her nakedness.

They were fifty stories up in his penthouse. They had been here for the last two days order room service and devouring each other. They'd been trying to strike a deal. She had been good, very good, the best.

Annie turned and smiled offering him one of the glasses of mimosa sitting on the ledge of the balcony. She lifted the other glass and raised it. The crystal sang a melody as the glasses kissed. He took a sip and looked out at the city before letting his eyes meet hers.

"What are you thinking about? " Paul asked.

"My virginity," she said in almost a whisper.

Paul chuckled as he tweaked one of her nipples.

"Do you wish not to be chaste?"

"Chaste?" she sniffed, "I will strike the shepherd and the flock shall be scattered…"

Paul took another taste of his cocktail and asked, "What does that mean? "

She looked into his dark eyes and saw her own reflection there.

"It's from the Bible."

"In Matthew, Jesus predicts Peter's denial. My most prized possession was swallowed by lust and I deemed it worthless ever since. Denying myself anything other than lust. Even Judas deemed the silver coins worthless after realizing his betrayal of innocence. It is by my deeds that I strip away my own character."

Paul and Annie stared into each other's eyes. Neither of them blinked. Paul finally smiled.

"It's not the translation of the Bible as much as it is the interpretation of the Bible. That's why you have so many different versions of one book."

He smiled and sipped.

"Did you know that virgin was a title given to a group of women living in those times? Mary was considered of this group. She had made a pledge to marry Joseph in an arranged ceremony set up by their parents as so many marriages were back in those times. Love wasn't even a consideration. When Joseph came to claim her, she was already with child."

He looked at her to see if she was really listening. She reached out and began stroking him staring into his eyes. He had her full attention and she had his.

"Joseph was obviously over taken by his own lust to shield Mary's innocence. Follow me. Jesus has been called the Son of Man, the Son of God; but never the son of Joseph. If a bastard child is a miracle than the ghetto is a glorious place. And your innocence hasn't been betrayed, it's been befriended. What a friend we have in Jesus. "

He sipped again and smacked a palm against Annie's buttocks. She looked at Paul and smiled continuing to stroke. She watched as the smile on his lips disappeared. His eyes started to water. He rubbed at his eye with his knuckle. He set the glass on the table and rubbed at his eyes. A smile crept to her lips. He opened his mouth to speak but no words came out. He grabbed at his chest and stumbled backward reaching for her. She placed a palm on his chest and guided him into one of the balcony chairs.

She straddled him as his chest heaved. She slid down on his hard cock and leaned close to his ear.

"Calm now, baby. It will all be over soon. Just try to enjoy your last moments. Not many get to die this way. I'm gonna tell them how good you were. How we were planning our honey moon. How we were celebrating our marriage and you died a happy man. Ssssss… ummm. Get off, baby."

Annie began to bounce up and down on his stiff member. She could hear her juices and see his chest heaving. She felt him shoot inside her. His chest stopped heaving at the same time his heart did.

Annie returned to the penthouse and retrieved some papers from her bag. She slipped on a pair of surgical gloves and went to the desk where the signature stamp was and stamped Paul's signature on the new documents. She picked up the old papers and the stamp and put them into a steel waste basket. She took the small waste basket out to the balcony and set the papers and stamp on fire. She closed the penthouse doors as the smoke billowed out over the city.

She looked at Paul sitting in the chair. The veins in his eyes were popped and his mouth hung open. His penis was still leaking. She thought about taking some pictures with her camera phone. She could release them on the internet in a few days. *Scandal*, she thought with a smile.

After the fire burned out, she emptied remnants into the toilet and flushed. She watched as her old life twirled in the water and disappeared. She wondered what Trey's reaction would be when he found out who his new boss was. She had so much to do.

She walked back into the room and made the 911 call. Everything played out just as she had planned it. The pills she had slipped in the drink had done the trick. Paul's death was classified heart attack. The EMS and detectives that showed up at the penthouse could barely do their job as Annie walked around in her birthday suit going to pieces over her husband's death.

She thought about the record producer, the one who had raped her on the studio floor so many years ago while his friends watched. He let them have a go at her while he taped it. That was before she was somebody when she was still a girl with hope and a dream even after all she had been through. They had stolen her dream that day.

The producer was washed up now but Annie was about to revive his career. She would get him and all of his friends. Then, she was going to find Roy because he had stolen her mother.

ANNIE O.
MURDER SHE WROTE
THE MIXTAPE COMING SOON…

George Sherman Hudson, CEO
Shawna A., COO

Thrust into the realities of life at a young age, Nikki uses what she knows and what her two older hoodrat friends, Katasha and FatFat, have taught her to survive.

Seeing no future in Chicago, Nikki heads to Atlanta with big dreams and a price on her head. Arriving in Atlanta she looks for a D-Boy to help her on her mission. What started off as a business partnership for her and Prime, turned into a ride-or-die relationship. Everything was lovely on the homefront until the Feds stepped in. Now Nikki is going all out to get the money needed to bring her man back home. Nikki gets the help she needs but what starts out as help, quickly turns to an obsession.

After Prime returns, he and Nikki settle back into their old life until her past comes back to haunt her and all hell breaks loose. Now her and Prime are faced with a tough decision...kill or be killed.

Love, fear and closely guarded secrets rule the hearts of four friends. When circumstances and unexpected events unfold the hidden truths, will the love dispel the fear? Or will the secrets breed a hatred that ultimately crushes and destroys every bond they have built between them?

Take a walk through the dark pages of "Tainted" and find out why loyalty is everything and betrayal carries the penalty of death.

We'd like to thank you for supporting G Street Chronicles
and invite you to join our social networks.
Please be sure to post a review when you're finished reading.

Like us on Facebook
G Street Chronicles
G Street Chronicles CEO Exclusive Readers Group

Follow us on Twitter
@GStreetChronicl

Follow us on Instagram
gstreetchronicles

Email us and we'll add you to our mailing list
fans@gstreetchronicles.com

George Sherman Hudson, CEO
Shawna A., COO